SLIM AND THE BEAST

INKSHARES

SAN FRANCISCO

SLIM AND
THE BEAST

A NOVEL

SAMUEL L. BARRANTES

For the Boys

To be sure, a human being is a finite thing, and his freedom is restricted. It is not freedom from conditions, but it is freedom to take a stand toward the conditions.

— Viktor Frankl

Slim's Famous Burger:

Lettuce, coleslaw, sliced tomatoes, a burger patty, American cheese, avocados, a second patty, a fried egg, ketchup, and hot sauce, Texas Pete to be precise.

SLIM AND THE BEAST

1

I'm going to tell you about a man named Slim. Who he is isn't important. It's who he was that matters now. Back before your eye pads and blue tooths and tweeting pages, not too long ago but long enough to make a difference, if you wanted to get to know someone, it was through honest conversation, not with smileys or emoticons. The only kindle was to light a fire, the nicest cell phone was called a razor, and even though Facebook existed you couldn't avoid sitting down for a drink. During that first decade of this here century, relationships took time and strayed away from brevity. You went to bars for civilization, whatever that was, maybe some music and a bit of whiskey. You could go for other reasons too, but only the loneliest of folk hoped to be seen.

Not that Slim was one to shy away from attention, but he was self-conscious on account of his scar. He'd taken a bullet through the jugular during Operation Iraqi Freedom, but lost faith in the cause during his second tour. He'd grown up as the afterthought of a deadbeat mother and spent his formative years at Stoke Ridge Military Academy, where the pedophiliacally-inclined Sgt. Chandler Dykes obsessed over Slim's naked torso and the other cadets' sturdy frames. But all in good time, as a wicked witch once said. Suffice to say Slim didn't enjoy his time at Stoke Ridge, not the least 'cause Sgt. Dykes was particularly fond of the skinny kid with a sharp tongue and a proclivity for aggression. Dykes also had a tendency toward self-pity, abusing Slim, and drinking Johnny Walker in the bathtub; he may not have taken baths with his cadets, but I'd venture to say he thought about it a few times. See, Dykes was fond of convincing young teenage boys to do shirtless pushups in his office, late night. He didn't abuse 'em in a sexual way, at least I don't think, but it remains a sign of the times that most scars have to be seen. And though Slim left Stoke Ridge with plenty of physical scars, they didn't keep him up at night like Sgt. Dykes's brutality.

But if I'm going to tell you about Slim, I've got to take Dykes's scars into account too. These were deep and invisible—more engrained, somehow. See, he used Slim and the other cadets—"Dykes's Tykes" as he called 'em, a well-toned troupe of at-risk youth—to help quell his demons, watching them pump out more shirtless pushups than any cared to count. Under the insectan buzz of a fluorescent light, Slim often fell asleep in Dykes's office, too exhausted to move from the stale carpet. And while the sergeant enjoyed all of his tykes, he was particularly fond of the skinny kid with a single name. Maybe it's 'cause Slim seemed to enjoy doing pushups, or perhaps 'cause he had a kind of fight about him; but whatever the reason, Dykes became obsessed, and it wasn't until the *Welcome Back Heroes!* event when Slim was nineteen, in that barren town of Stoke Ridge, NC—the town's main attraction being a brick building with a white steeple—that this

story either commenced or drew to a close, depending on your pref-
erence for happy endings.

The *Welcome Back Heroes!* event was a sign of things to come, for
it was the day Slim reached the top of Sgt. Dykes's B.A.M. LIST. The
Belligerents According to Me list, filled with the names of Dykes's
mother, father, and other supposed enemies from his fallow past,
was first displayed in his Stoke Ridge office (which, according to
Slim, smelled like an unkempt microwave) and was later hung in
the sergeant's home off Exit 263, in a one-story cabin with a rickety
screen door, built on a once-fertile piece of land that's now hardened
earth and brown grass.

"Welcome back, son," Dykes said.

Just a few days prior Slim had been in Iraq. The white bandage
around his neck had to be changed every evening. He stood with his
hands held behind his back, accepting an award for *Outstanding Service
to the Stoke Ridge Community and Nation as a Whole.* The auditorium was
packed. A true hero's welcome.

"Congratulations on your medal." Dykes faked a smile and spoke
into the mic. "Now state your name and rank, son. Good to have
you back."

Dykes stuck out his hand. Slim didn't reciprocate. "I ain't your son,
Chandler. Give me the mic."

They stood on an elevated stage in the middle of the basketball
court. Dykes's voice bounced off the bannerless rafters. Chairs scuffed
the floor and leaned on the back wall. The aluminum roofing rejected
the echoes, sending them back down to the podium where Slim took
control of the stage.

"What a pleasure it is, what a pleasure it is." Slim shook the
sergeant's hand and gripped it tightly. "Seeing you slaving away

behind the mic like that? I thought I'd never see you again, Chandler Dykes . . ."

Dykes was upset. Slim had now called him by his first name twice. "*Name and rank* son—and you address me as *sergeant.*"

"I'm a war hero now," Slim laughed. "More than you can say for yourself. Careful now Dykes. You don't want that forehead vein popping out . . ."

Dykes laughed nervously, trying to distract the audience. He put his arm around Slim as if it were a friendly conversation, turning away from the mic to say something in private. And whatever Dykes whispered, Slim fell silent. Dykes turned back to the audience with a yellow-toothed smile.

"Sorry about that folks. Technical issues. Now give it up for Slim— the hero of Iraq!"

The audience applauded but they did not roar. Dykes tried to corral Slim. Slim didn't abide.

"Get your goddamn hands off of me," Slim said into the mic.

Dykes's face twitched. The audience squirmed. And perhaps knowing their history, or perhaps 'cause he liked the spotlight, the academy's director—a bear of a man by the name of General Haith, who'd die in a house fire a few years down the line—scrambled onto the stage, took Slim's place on the podium, positioned his broad shoulders between Slim and Sgt. Dykes, and laughed loudly. The mic gave feedback. The video footage corroborates it. A child in the front row stuck his fingers in his ears; other spectators squinted at the stage as if staring at the sun, wincing from the feedback as they waited for what came next.

"Let's give it up for Slim!" General Haith boomed. "Our hometown hero. Maybe the finest soldier we've ever had!"

The tension escaped the gymnasium amidst the clapping and the noise, after which General Haith proceeded to give a long-winded speech about what-it-means-to-be-a-member-of-the-Stoke-Ridge-community-and-how-it's-men-like-these-that-define-our-nation-et-cetera-etcetera. Now you might be wondering how Slim got himself onto that stage, and though the details are unimportant (at least for now), the whole hoo-ha surrounding his return was mostly 'cause of his reputation as a formidable killing machine. See, when Slim started at Stoke Ridge he was a string bean cadet, a timid child without much physical promise: chicken legs and noodly arms and a chest that was vacuum-packed. Slim's mother, Wilhelmina Jenkins (who we'll get to), was a drug addict who subsisted on reheated Hot Pockets, hardened Kraft mac n' cheese, and frozen mozzarella sticks. As a child, Slim always looked a bit sickly, always scrounging for food in the cupboards lest he be forced to reheat something in the moldy microwave, but by the time GW Bush decided to play his daddy's game, Slim had become the finest warrior Stoke Ridge had ever seen. Of course, Slim never knew his dad, but he must've benefited from some hunk's formidable genes; though his hairline was receding by the time he was eighteen, his six-foot-five frame, accompanied by four years of bursting biceps and peck muscles filled out on four hundred plus pushups a day, made the man quite a sight to behold. His newfound body led to his award for bravery in Iraq during the First Battle of Fallujah—a hell of a fight for those boys in the red, white, and blue—for killing an entire platoon of alleged al-Qaeda operatives and taking a bullet straight through the jugular. And while the doctors said it was a miracle he'd survived, Slim said it was a miracle they'd gotten him out before he could reload his M60. He was a hero of sorts (as far as modern war heroes go), but warriors these days are often shamed and quickly forgotten.

"And this man right here," General Haith said as he put his arm around Slim at the podium, "we'll never forget what he's done for us!"

The crowd applauded. Sgt. Dykes didn't. Once again Slim took back the mic.

"Or else," Slim remarked, "those bastards would've felt a wrath they hadn't experienced since Genghis Khan came at them with his hordes! I'm not done, mark my words: I'm gonna get back there. Just wait and see."

A few audience members gasped. A few others cheered. Many were confused 'cause they thought Genghis Khan was some kind of ethnic dish.

"That's right," Slim continued. "Unlike some of us, I'm willing to fight! I don't just sit in my office all day watching kids do pushu—."

Dykes grabbed the mic. "Thank you for that Slim. How about another round of applause?"

While there were some grumblings in the audience about what Slim was talking about, the crowd cheered nonetheless 'cause that's what crowds do. After Dykes was unable to answer any questions about the war, Slim took back the podium. "As you can tell, I learned to fight once people started shooting at me. But as far as Stoke Ridge goes? Well, let's just say I didn't learn much at all . . ."

Sgt. Dykes bit his fingernails. His fake smile faltered.

"The thing is, it's not hard to develop fatherless kids into killers," Slim said. He was laid back and confident. "And now we're the ones killing fathers in Iraq. Of course, a lot of these officers," Slim looked directly at Dykes, "don't have to do any killing at all, right? They only know about sending us boys out there while they sit behind simulators with whiskey and whack off."

General Haith blushed. Dykes tried to take control of the mic again but Slim managed to push him off. "Most of 'em, like Dykes here, have never been to Iraq. They can give us orders, sure. But then they all just sit back with their hands behind their head like they're getting some kind of patriotic blow job."

The audience fell silent. Flies buzzed around the gym. A squirrel or a cat scampered across the aluminum roof. Slim sneered at Dykes and the military brass, handing General Haith the mic as he stepped back. The general quelled the situation by bringing up freedom and the good fight, and after a final round of hesitant applause, brown-fatigued cadets escorted the spectators onto the brown lawn, where sweet tea and lemonade were served in red plastic cups. As for what happened next, there are only two people who know the story, and neither Slim nor Sgt. Dykes ever told me exactly. Whatever it was, it was violent and quick. Slim almost died. Here are the facts:

After hearing a commotion in Dykes's office, a group of cadets found Slim writhing on the floor, clutching his jugular, gurgling in agony. A crimson fountain spurted from the wound—the sergeant had tried to pop Slim's Adam's apple like bubble wrap. Dykes was right beside him, curled up on the bloodstained floor, whispering the same phrase to himself over and over again: "Never listening. Never playing. Never so much as a goddamned hug. Never listening. Never playing. Never so much as a goddamned hug." As soon as the cadets piled on top of Dykes, he began to thrash and kick around, breaking noses and shattering adolescent bones. Slim would've died if it hadn't been for General Haith, who came in just in time to apply pressure to the wound. By the time Slim arrived at the hospital he'd lost over three pints of blood. He remained in a coma for three straight weeks and spent another month on heavy morphine drip. General Haith was there every day to check on the young war hero; even though Slim was unconscious, the general stayed by his side. If you're wondering why, your guess is as good as mine; maybe it was 'cause General Haith felt responsible, or maybe it was 'cause he hated Sgt. Dykes.

It took two surgeries and three months to rewire Slim's vocal chords, but Slim kept his promise and soon returned to Iraq. As for Dykes, after being treated for three cracked ribs and a pierced eardrum, he was released. Needless to say, the attack effectively ended Dykes's career. And while Slim wouldn't file any charges 'cause this is the military we're talking about, he did acquire a five-year restraining order, more than enough time, he thought, to get Dykes out of his life. In later years, Slim told me putting Dykes in prison wasn't an option: no one could prove who started the fight, technically Slim's neck was already wounded (and so it could be deemed an unfortunate accident), and the military is one of the best in the business when it comes to protecting its own during a scandal. Still, Dykes didn't get off easy. When he returned home that night, his relationship with Slim forever tarnished, Stoke Ridge's former prom kings and defensive linemen were waiting for him on his front lawn. The attack had been the final straw, in a sense: what with his nasal voice, puppy dog eyes, and proclivity for whiskey and young cadets, most of Stoke Ridge didn't take kindly to the sergeant. Upon seeing the angry mob, Dykes somehow managed to sneak in the back door. He spent the evening in a locked bathroom, drinking Johnny Walker in the bathtub, and cried himself to sleep in a naked fetal position. The following day he awoke to General Haith's voice on a loudspeaker—Dykes had exactly one hour to get out of town. With his bags packed but not ready to go, Dykes began driving away in his rusty brown pickup, leaving only the second home he'd ever known. On his way out of Stoke Ridge he passed three burning effigies and a mob of angry townspeople. They threw cups of iced tea at his windshield and old basketballs under his car. One man used a baseball bat to smash a side-mirror and another shot out his break lights with an assault rifle. As Dykes watched the church steeple fade in the rearview mirror, his car thumping forward, the back tire slowly losing air (metal shards), he felt like vomiting and crying at the same time, which is exactly what he did off Exit 263.

For a time, while Slim recovered and prepared to fight once more, Dykes lived as a vagrant, seeking refuge in homeless shelters and the occasional motel, where he often slept naked with Johnny Walker. Though Slim faired better, it wasn't by much: during his second tour in Iraq he became distraught and disillusioned, not unlike the sergeant after the award ceremony. Still, Slim tried to move on while Dykes impatiently waited for his return.

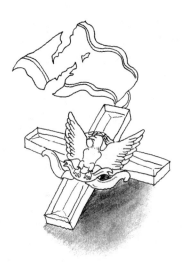

2

The scar was centered on Slim's Adam's apple, white around the edges, the middle slightly pink. It would take him three years to be able to look at it in the mirror and one more year to confidently shave under his neck. He went through speech therapy to recover his Southern drawl, but once the scar tissue healed and his voice came back—slightly gruffer now, more serious to match his eyes—Slim boarded a troop transport destined for Iraq, fully bearded with a clean-shaved head.

Being abroad, he later told me, somehow made him feel more connected, maybe 'cause he'd never known what it was to feel at home. But the second time around wouldn't result in any fanfare, and though his trigger-finger received the Distinguished Service Cross, he'd return a pariah in the media's eyes, blacklisted by the military for refusing to follow orders.

What happened was, Slim had been up in a Black Hawk helicopter doing surveillance work—a reconnaissance flight over Baghdad—when he received an order to fire on a terrorist convoy. Slim knew it was nothing more than a couple school buses 'cause he'd worked with one of the schoolteachers just the day before. But his commanding officer told him it was al-Qaeda, goddammit, and if Slim knew what was good for him he'd blast 'em. And so when some "jackass behind a computer screen" (Slim's words, not mine) said one of the terrorists (teachers) was carrying a weapon (a camera), Slim disarmed his M60 before watching in horror as the kids succumbed to a drone. Fifty-six children died in the attack. It was enough for Slim to take his dog tags off there and then. He didn't wait until landing to disown the military, submitting his resignation by tossing his dog tags out the helicopter. After ridiculing and threatening to imprison Slim, the brass decided to send him home lest he tell the truth about what went wrong. They knew Slim was justified—they'd made the mistake of killing thousands of kids before—but the last thing the military wanted was more bad news. Even though Slim filed a complaint and refused to back down, he was easily silenced. The government chalked it up to an alleged drug problem and a faulty drone.

"Sometimes . . . well yes, I know about his report," a spokesperson said. "But he's been through a lot. He doesn't have his head screwed on just right. Have you seen his scar? Of cour—well of course it's tragic, Susan. I have kids too. But you know what Susan? Sometimes robots make mistakes."

And so Slim returned a disenfranchised war hero, allegedly addicted to cocaine or heroine or crack. The government was quick to discredit any stories he might tell. His face showed up in regional papers that blamed him for the fifty-six dead children. His mother had been addicted to weed (yes, it's possible) and they used this to drive the point home—high as a kite up in a helicopter, Slim was a loose cannon. One magazine spun it as: "CRACK, THE SILENT WAR:

PORTRAIT OF A KILLER." Mysterious bags of cocaine also began showing up at Slim's motel room (he tried to stay out of the limelight), and even if the authorities had no proof, well, the government has a way of outsourcing personal grudges. His mother wasn't there to greet him at the airport 'cause she was too high or too insensitive to care that he was gone, so Slim returned home angry and alone, unable to confide in anyone about his experience. Derided by townsfolk and regional news teams, and vowing never to return to Stoke Ridge Military Academy, the twenty-year-old found solace for the summer in the North Carolina countryside, holed up in a Motel 6, smoking weed under the cicada-filled pines.

A change soon came, as all changes do. Thanks to the GI Bill (even if the funds weren't really enough), Slim enrolled at the University of North Carolina. He saved money for the fall by selling the cocaine that showed up at his motel room to addicts who always called and never knocked. But what with the death threats from military folk who didn't know the difference between patriotism and war and a mysterious masked man who clumsily kept trying to frame Slim out in the open, one time throwing a dime bag through the second-story window of his hotel, another time pulling up at a stoplight and doing just the same, Slim kept to himself as much as he could, counting down the days until his new life could start. When he moved to UNC Chapel Hill, he wasn't so much forgotten as ignored: the conservative kids didn't trust him 'cause he'd spoken out against the war, while the liberals scoffed at his "heroism." Those who knew about his past feared his neck scar, and those who didn't equated him with some type of ex-military drug addict. At least, Slim later told me, the rumors helped him focus on his studies. Though it remained a mystery to virtually everyone who knew him, Slim found refuge in the comforts of his own mind. See, as a child he loved to read his mom's coffee-table books, *The Far Side* and *Calvin and Hobbes*. He had never been pushed in school, but finally at UNC he could study what he wanted. "When everything's gone to shit," he once said, "there's nothing to pull you out of the hole like a bit of Jung or Rilke." Content with his books on philosophy and theory, Slim learned how to be happy and alone. And though he was paranoid for a time and had occasional nightmares about Sgt. Dykes, he didn't care how cocaine kept finding its way into his gym locker. He chalked it up to someone in the military brass and took advantage of the dime bags; he never did snort the stuff, but made a killing selling to frat boys and sorority girls who used the stuff to study for the MCAT and LSAT and other acronymic exams. He only went to parties if he could peddle the drugs, which continued to appear throughout his sophomore year. He loved flirting with women but did fine without 'em just the same, and he couldn't have cared less about UNC's famous basketball team. After a sophomore year that saw two successful semesters but a near miss with campus police (they'd seen Slim speaking to a black kid in an alley and figured they were up to no good), Slim stopped selling to strangers and moved into his own place off Rosemary Street, a small white house with a brown roof and a leaky kitchen faucet that reminded him of his childhood home.

Finally able to look in the mirror without thinking of Sgt. Dykes, Slim finished his junior year on the dean's list, having spent his time in the library ensconced in social theory. He had no real friends and preferred the solitude of his studies to the social platitudes; and though he would've liked to share his feelings with a friend or two, he didn't think anyone wanted to philosophize or discuss. Or maybe it was an excuse to avoid something deeper, 'cause despite his smooth talking, drug dealing, and laudable grades, Slim didn't believe he was worthy of conversation. He kept his eyes on a future he couldn't quite envision, and paid his tuition with the GI Bill and the mysterious bags of cocaine. If someone were trying to frame him, so be it, he thought. The truth was there was a part of him that wanted to be found out. For what, he wasn't sure, but he felt like a phony—not like Holden Caulfield, but in an emptier way. So as summer thunderstorms began to roll in over the Piedmont, inviting Slim to read on the porch and listen to the rain, he never raised his head to notice the brown pickup down the street concealed behind a willow tree, the driver going insane.

3

Dykes was a *watcher*. He never would have used the word *stalk*. Of course, Slim wasn't the only one Dykes kept an eye on—throughout the years there'd been other cadets, too—but Slim reminded Dykes of himself somehow, and so Slim remained at the top of the B.A.M. LIST. In front of the computer screen, Dykes lived vicariously, fostering a connection to Slim that in reality he'd never known. Not that Slim had a Facebook—let's just say the government didn't allow it—but there were plenty of pictures from his time out there in Iraq. And so Dykes scanned the Internet for Slim's hardened face. It didn't make him happier, of course, but by obsessing over his cadets' former lives, by commenting on their digital appearance until they blocked him, by trying to start debates about subjects that weren't his own, Dykes understood his digital friendships as something profound, spending most of his days online, forever connected, forever alone.

He'd been born sometime in 1976. His mother's name was Sasha and she didn't keep her maiden name. She was a sociable, voluptuous woman who'd never slept in a single bed. She liked shiny things and enjoyed catered caviar. Dykes's father was named Trent and he sweated profusely; short-tempered with a strong jaw but fatty face, he had a receding hairline and a nasal voice. He never told his wife he loved her, but he frequently slapped her ass.

"That's where I get it from," Dykes told me one night at my bar. "My dad always had that film above his lip. He smelled like something sour, slightly rotten, something fierce. He liked things that looked expensive. That's why he married my mom."

Chandler Dykes wiped his forehead with a translucent napkin. This was only the second time I'd ever talked to him. "They only thought about themselves. And maybe that's what they saw in each other. What's the word, Lockart?"

"I don't know, Chandler. You're gonna need to give me more than that."

"It's a guy above a pond?"

"You mean Narcissus?"

"No, it's something else. But my mom spent most days there, down by the pond. That's what I mean. Thinking about her art as she called it. I never understood it, to be honest. Seemed like something to pass the time. But my dad was always working. He stayed in his air-conditioned office. My mom always visited at the end of the month. I only went in there once. It had mahogany doors and a red carpet, too. He had one of those desks with open leg space under it . . ."

Dykes's tone changed. He pulled at the tuft on his receding hairline. "Are you a family man, Lockart?"

"Why yes indeed, I am." I held up my left hand.

"Right, I'm so stupid. I'm sure she's beautiful."

"Yes, she is."

"You're a lucky man, Lockart. And a good husband, right?"

"Well I'd like to think so, yes. We all have our moments."

"You never ask her to do things, do you? You don't have a list of all the others, right?"

"All the others? On a list? Are we still talking about my wife?"

Dykes shuddered. "Lucky man, Lockart. A family man. Gosh. You know I had a nephew once?"

"I'm sorry to hear that."

"What? No he's still alive . . . I just haven't seen him in a while. It's been years now, actually. But here, I have a picture."

Dykes raised his buttocks off the barstool and pulled out an engorged wallet from his back pocket. "Here, take a look at him. That's him. He's cute, right?"

Dykes showed me a Polaroid of a teenage boy. He was standing ankle-deep in a pool of water, holding up a fishing net full of live crawdads. The boy's eyes smiled but his mouth was unfazed. Something about his regard made me feel pity.

"Such a good kid. Used to call me Uncle Chandler. Uncle Sarge."

"But not anymore?"

"He ran away from home, that's all."

Much like their son, Dykes's parents drank heavily most nights, which soon melded into their daily routines. At night the excuse was catered parties. Being beautiful and/or rich was enough to suffice in Chapel Hill's community of nouveau riche, where it wasn't uncommon for middle-aged white people to be genuinely surprised that the Latino waiter had a master's. But Sasha and Trent were mostly just ignorant, blinded by the light from the chandelier's glare bouncing off fine jewelry and porcelain Botoxed faces, so that employing minorities for a catering service was both praiseworthy and progressive in their squinting eyes. They didn't see many ethnicities out in the North Carolina countryside, most of the residents being hospitable, wrinkled folk who may or may not recognize the problem with a Confederate flag.

The Dykeses lived out in the country near the town of Efland, off Old 86 where no two houses look the same. It was (and still is, if I recall) a land of fields and meadows, tick-infested forests, and rusted dry creeks, where old tanks of propane surround dilapidated gas stations, where the landscape is landmarked by hay bales and cows, where a smoothly paved road is a chance for respite, where the farmland isn't lonely but can make you feel alone, and where driving at night demands a strong pair of headlights and a discerning eye for suicidal deer. Out there it was easy to get lost—capture-the-flag, flashlight tag, and hide-and-seek were king—but Chandler Dykes knew none of it 'cause he didn't have friends growing up. He never saw a bonfire and the only time he had a picnic was when he ate granola bars in the woods. Dogs barked at him. Cats never rubbed up on his leg. Even though they hissed, Dykes was enamored with opossums. He didn't know about hushpuppies or sweet tea or Cheerwine, and he could count on one hand the number of times he'd had chicken and dumplings. But according to tax forms, bank accounts, and grocery receipts, Chandler Dykes was a privileged child. He grew up in a wooden house designed by a New York architect, a man who had a proclivity for bay windows, high ceilings, and eagle's nests. Light cascaded into the three-story mansion, which was filled with glass tables, smooth objects, and expensive bowls from countries with names no one knew how to pronounce. They collected wealth but didn't use it. They even had a cooking island. There was a sauna in the west wing and a hot-tubbed balcony in the south, neither of which was used more than twice. Chandler lived in a loft, ten feet above his hardwood-floored bedroom, where he spent his days watching soap operas. Sometimes he watched geese and other birds pass by the bay windows, which were cleaned once a week by a man on a rope whose name was Jesus. Chandler's father hated immigrants but loved under-paying them: Mexican, Colombian, and Nicaraguan migrant workers often tended the twenty acres of land, trimming hedges, mowing grass, marking trees with pink tags. Of course, Trent Dykes never stepped foot in the forest or took a dip in the pond and would only do business with the Jefe. Sasha was kinder to the caretakers, occasionally saying "Hola señor," giggling in her polka-dot dress by the pond.

"I never really knew what she was doing down there," Dykes recounted. He sat on the edge of his barstool, hovering over the bar. "Wading around, setting up a camera on the far side. There was a structure there, made of wood. Kind of like a diving board? And she'd climb up and look down in the water, where she'd placed those oil containment booms, like the ones used for oil spills. She filled the sections with different colored paint, but in all the years I watched her she never jumped, not once. She just stood there up top, peering down toward the painted pond."

While Sasha refused to jump, Trent threw catered parties. Chandler's early years were defined by buxom female waitresses serving boat-shoed Southern boys and diamond-studded women. The men smoked cigars and drank whiskey. The women took champagne, hard lemonade, and mojitos. They conversed about vacation homes and family pedigree. A lot of the guests assumed Sasha was successful 'cause she never shared her art. Never allowed to go downstairs in the evening, Chandler stayed upstairs and surveyed the scene below, his father swaying from side to side, ogling the waitstaff and escorting them behind a shed next to the pond. "It was always out behind the wood shed, on the far side of the pond. She always got down on her knees, this one caterer named

Eve. My dad ran his fingers across her scalp. My mom knew, right? She must've known. But she just schmoozed with her artist friends and pretended not to notice. But she was a concept artist, you know? It was all about the idea. But if you want my opinion she didn't even know *how* to make art."

Chandler grew used to sitting atop his perch, staring through the bay windows at his parents' life down below. "There's something empowering about being above it all," he said. The truth was Chandler Dykes wasn't above any of it, just that the loneliness of the loft instilled a sense of superiority in the young child. At four years old he was talking back in earnest and by six he was outright insulting his mom. He called her stupid for letting Daddy and Eve be naughty, and whenever Sasha cried, Trent beat his son with a wooden rod. Yet the most egregious of the Dykeses' parenting errors was that they were never around. Instead, Dykes was more or less raised at the YMCA. The Young Men's Christian Association (which Trent Dykes often criticized for being neither youthful, manly, nor Christian) was Chandler Dykes's asylum. Since Trent worked late and Sasha spent her days by the pond, they reasoned it would be easier to pay off the Y and not raise him at all. And so it was there that Chandler learned to watch his peers, mostly young adolescent boys, exercise in the weight room. Though the YMCA staff's kindness might've been dishonest (being paid for in cash), they bought Little Chandler Gatorades and made him feel at home. One trainer named Tim taught him how to do pushups, and another helped him with his biceps and said Chandler had nice arms. YMCA became Dykes's place of worship, where he lost himself in the mist of the groin sweat and the grunting and the swimming pool's chlorinated sounds. It was here that he learned to love the heavy breathing, the strained grunts, the "give me twenties" and squeaking sneakers, the stoic pain that comes with working out.

He'd sit in the lobby by the vending machines, watching kids from the local high schools run on treadmills. He'd stand on his tippy-toes on the bench in the lobby—the kind with a blue cushion and the yellow foam ripped out—and press his nose up to the glass window to watch kids strain under an incandescent light. His favorite moment (aside from watching the bench presses and the wall sits and the pushups) was when the kids finished their workout and patted him on the head: Little Chandler, they called him. Little Tyke.

Dykes was surely thinking about all of this and more as he sat in his brown pickup and spied on Slim. It was June 2009, months before senior year, but Slim wasn't on a lake drinking beers in the sun, he was reading nonfiction alone on his porch. Dykes was hoping to break in when Slim went out—he wanted to steal something important—but it seemed that the more he watched, the less Slim left the house. But Dykes had grown used to waiting for things that never came. At least in his mind it gave him a chance to plan. The following year, upon Slim's graduation, he would have his vengeance. Dykes spent his days in his pickup and his nights at my bar, lamenting his past. He spent his weekends at the corner table, scanning Facebook and at times talking to himself about the loneliness of Dykes Pond, where his mother had waded in her polka-dot dress while Trent harassed tight-skirted interns in his air-conditioned office. As he'd done on more nights than I care to count, Dykes finished his drunken evenings with the Polaroid at the bar. "My nephew, just look at him. What a good tyke. Did I tell you he used to call me Uncle Sarge?"

As usual, Dykes asked if he could take some peanuts home for Lenny. "And do you have any ziplock bags? I just ran out of motel plastic shower caps."

I poured the remnants of the bar nuts into Dykes's cupped hands.

"It's for Lenny, you know? He loves peanuts, that's all."

4

It's a shame college athletes don't have a right to their own name, and the all-American Hugh Dawton-Fields, aka The Beast, was of course no exception. One look at the young man and you'd be hard pressed to come up with a better nickname. He was seven feet two on his tippy-toes—size-nineteen feet, the biggest in the NCAA—and 290 pounds after a full meal. His hands were the size of frying pans, his wingspan about seven feet six. Standing under the ten-foot hoop, The Beast could touch the rim without even straining. He had bulging biceps, massive forearms, and a chest that often got in the way. He entered most rooms sideways. One player described him as a seven-foot freight train. But as our man Slim would soon learn, the expression "appearances can be deceiving," though trite and overused, was particularly true when it came to The Beast.

Hugh Dawton-Fields's portrait was painted by secondary acquaintances, sports writers who thought they knew him, and fans who

believed they knew why he played basketball. They thought they understood why he didn't like the spotlight; but even if he was shy, reasons
aren't the same as explanations. As a kid he was taunted for being tall,
lanky, and quiet. When he went through puberty in early high school,
he was made fun of just the same. He was a dominant, forceful player,
but a frustrated one. Not used to his newfound size of a staggering
six feet eight at sixteen, in high school he had trouble controlling his
strength, breaking more than a few noses and wrists along the way.
On account of his playing style, he usually ended up on the bench at
the end of the game. He didn't mind it though, watching the game
end from the sidelines. According to one scout he had the size but
lacked a passion; still, his averages spoke for themselves: 35.3 points,
21.5 rebounds, and 8.4 blocks, all while playing a little over half of
the game. After a high school career that eclipsed even Wilt "The
Stilt" Chamberlain's, The Beast entered UNC destined to become a
legend. In his first year he won ACC Freshman of the Year. During
his sophomore year he was a top-five all-American. Forever the quiet
one who distrusted the business side of things, Hugh Dawton-Fields
was a soft-spoken superstar, refusing all interviews, hiding in the locker
room after the game.

No one was able to crack The Beast's demeanor. Professional scouts
and well-dressed agents were baffled he didn't leave early for the
NBA. He was old school, if that still meant anything. Most believed
he loved the college game and the focus on team, but the truth was
his main goal was a college degree; and as long as UNC kept selling
tickets, only opponents found time to complain. What with all the
agents and hype surrounding such a dominant player, no one knew
or cared about the kid behind the nickname. He was polite and quiet
and always showed up to practice early; but he left on time just the
same. Some NBA scouts questioned his intensity. The Beast was a

superstar without the fanfare, a celebrity without the tabloids—if the kid known as Hugh Dawton-Fields were ever asked for an interview, that one might be granted; but UNC made too much money off the nickname (fans even petitioned to have it on the back of his jersey). And so he played more aggressively on account of the chants; he fouled more intentionally on account of the jeers; he screamed louder when he dunked on account of the TV and made a habit of fouling out at the end of games. On the court he was a phenom destined for the NBA, but off the court he refused to answer anyone who called him The Beast.

According to Sgt. Dykes, who said he'd done his research, everything came down to punching Assistant Coach Jim Brees. No one knows what Coach Brees said, but it most assuredly had to do with The Beast's parents' deaths: the punch came just three months after the family restaurant Chez Moi burned down, when The Beast returned to the hardwood in hopes of moving on. The only thing the media talked about was Jim Brees's near-death experience—neither Jim Brees nor The Beast ever spoke about what was said. It was as if The Beast's culpability was a foregone conclusion 'cause, like an NCAA spokesperson suggested, how could a respected Division I coach be in the wrong? One teammate said Coach Brees called The Beast a faggot for crying, for which The Beast picked him up by the armpits and slammed him to the ground before bloodying his face. A janitor watching from high up in the stadium said The Beast knocked Brees out without warning; but the most likely story is that of Alex Morgan, a curly-haired point guard who spent quite a lot of time on the bench. "I won't say what was said because I know what you'll do with it. But trust me when I say it was out of place. He was running suicides, just like the rest of us. Coach Brees got in Hugh's face for falling behind. Some words were exchanged and Hugh asked Coach

Brees to repeat it. Coach did and Hugh backhanded him right across the face [. . .] No, he deserved it. That's my opinion at least. [. . .] It wasn't a punch, it was a backhand." Even if Alex Morgan's story is to be believed, verbal abuse was no excuse for almost rendering a coach blind. There were plenty of debates on ESPN and talk radio about what *could have been said* and if it even mattered, and if it did, *what did he say?* and if he did say it, *why?* But The Beast refused to speak about it and Coach Brees seemed too scared. Whatever the case, The Beast was immediately expelled from the team and potentially the university; though he'd been suspended before, it had been for an in-game ejection (nose breaking), and it's one thing for the powers that be to pull strings for flagrant fouls or the occasional bloodied face, but putting a staff member in a coma for three weeks? This was a serious offense that no PR expert or hoity-toity academic could right fix. Lest The Beast's story end prematurely, the sentencing judge—an adamant basketball fan who had high hopes for The Beast saved Hugh Dawton-Fields from expulsion by sentencing him to five hundred hours of community service at The Skillet.

Now don't ask me how flipping burgers can be swung as punishment, but my guess is UNC wasn't ready to lose so much money. They'd spent three years selling THE BEAST T-shirts and Coca-Cola bottles—in short there were plenty of financial reasons to keep The Beast at UNC, including financing the athletic director's sixtieth birthday party. Putting The Beast in The Skillet was a good choice for the community as the mayor was hoping to clean up (gentrify) that side of town. And so under the buzz of an incandescent light, amidst the fumes of sizzling burger patties and golden-brown onions, where the only way to stretch his neck was to stick his head out of the cramped food truck, Hugh Dawton-Fields was able to lose himself in a task. No one dared to ask about Coach Brees or the sentencing 'cause The Beast was legally obligated to stay quiet (and was also over seven feet). Like all sports scandals most people forgot in a few weeks. But Slim was different. He wasn't much for nicknames.

The Skillet was just off of Franklin Street, Chapel Hill's most famous thoroughfare. Cutting through the university's verdant campus, the street is lined with upscale fast-food joints, souvenir shops, and boutiques. Turquoise blue T-shirts cover the backs of most inhabitants, and though the grounds of UNC are known for their classical beauty—grassy knolls and oak trees, white-columned frat houses, lush lawns in front of sororities—you don't have to walk far off of West Franklin to see what Chapel Hill used to be. The burger joint sat in an abandoned parking lot in what the academics called a rough area of town, which in student orientation seminars meant anything near Rosemary Street. This was the implied area to avoid when "straying off campus," even if in truth these neighborhoods were safer than most fraternities. In earlier decades there'd been murders, of course, but which American town hasn't seen its share of bloodshed? And sure, there were rusting homes with rustier bikes out front, and sad patches of brown grass congregating on the front lawns, but there were also little kids playing hopscotch in the street, avoiding tufts of grass sprouting out of the cracked concrete—it was more lived in, The Beast once said, and hence more alive. Chain-link fences cordoned the unpatrolled neighborhoods from the pristine grounds of UNC. Abandoned buildings loomed tall, failed investments rumored to be crack dens.

Some say it was just a guise to keep too many fans from trying to meet The Beast. Here, at the food truck that had no wheels, The Skillet made the best burger in the city, plain and simple. And though the golfing students from Pinehurst and horseback riders from Southern Pines avoided it 'cause they were afraid of interacting with poor kids, the surrounding neighborhoods were thrilled to come down and catch a glimpse of the nation's most fearsome ballplayer serving a beef patty.

Neighborhood kids came in droves to play soccer or toss a football in front of The Skillet, hoping to catch a glimpse of the famous man-child. He was a kid after all; what else can you be at eighteen? But he was a kid with a passion for cooking and was relieved to be away from the game. While plenty of people believed he was destined to become a legend, for a brief summer fans thought of him primarily as a chef. The truck without wheels had a low ceiling and a single light bulb that dangled from a string, which The Beast had to duck under each time he reached for more buns. When he turned to serve customers he had to watch out for his broad shoulders. Small red baskets with wax paper were stacked on the counter next to brown napkins. The Beast never served fries 'cause he believed they were cheap; he served baked potatoes, but not the kind with sour cream. He grilled onions and zucchinis and red peppers and green peppers. He sizzled grass-fed beef and free-range chickens and the occasional mango slice. There was a menu to order from 'cause most patrons weren't creative, but The Beast was adamant every time he greeted them: "If I've got the ingredients I can make it. What'll it be?" Compared to his physical and sometimes brutal playing style, The Beast had finesse behind the countertop. Customers admired the way he kept an egg's yoke from running and how he stacked each ingredient so that nothing fell off when you took a bite.

Of course, when Slim arrived he didn't sit back and watch 'cause he wanted to talk. He'd taken Adderall that morning to read through some dense theory; and even though he wasn't hungry, after ten hours he had to eat. Slim's Famous Burger, as it would come to be called—to this day you can order it from the chalkboard menu, though the writing is fading some and you really have to know it by heart—was served hundreds of times during that summer, not just to Slim, but to all the others who saw the light.

The day they met—let's call it mid-June 2009—Slim approached The Skillet's window and planted both hands on the countertop. "Hey man, I'm trying to eat. You think you can help me?" Slim was energized, a bit uppity.

The Beast was chopping onions and slicing mangoes. The skillet was sizzling. He didn't hear Slim.

"Well you gonna turn around there, Wilt? See I was thinking of getting a hammmmmburger—you think you can do that for me?"

The Beast didn't turn around immediately 'cause he assumed Slim was an annoying fan. He finished sautéing a few onions and then slowly turned to see who it could be.

"Yeah. Take a look at the menu." The Beast quickly returned to flipping a few patties. He assumed Slim, like most of the customers, had no imagination.

"Menu? What menu? I know what I want, all right. Do I look like someone who can't choose? I don't need a goddamn menu, you dig?"

The Beast turned around again. This was the first customer of the day. "Glad to hear it." The Beast smiled. "Write down what you want on this slip of paper. You can check the boxes for the ingredients—"

"Now hold up, Wilt," Slim interrupted. He put his hand out, as if to calm him. "I ain't checking no boxes on no goddamn piece of paper. I don't mean to be rude, but I've got a system, see? Now here's what's gonna happen, Wilt—can I call you Wilt?"

"No. You can call me Hugh."

"Hugh. Wilt. Same difference. You're tall like Wilt Chamberlain. You probably play like him, too. But okay, I'll call you Hugh. You're that famous ballplayer right? Yeah I thought so. Good. Now what I want is some tomatoes. But not them cubes like the Mexicans like 'em—I'm talking freshly cut circles. You think you can handle that for me? That okay with you, Hugh?"

"You want cheese on that?"

"Well *goddamnit* Hugh, you think I'm finished? No sir, I'm just getting started. Now don't get behind Hugh—I know it's hard to think from way up there, but we got some work to do, you dig? I'm gonna need some lettuce on it and avocados, too. Double burger. And coleslaw—give me some of that spread on top. You getting this? You sure you don't need to write this down? Making us check boxes . . . what kind of place is this? So we've got lettuce and tomatoes and we've got coleslaw. We've got avocados. We've got double burger patties . . . you still with me? Good. Now I'm also gonna need a fried egg on that, with a slice of American cheese on top."

"No problem. Is that it?"

"Are you in a hurry, Wil—I mean Hugh? You got a ballgame to get to or something? Don't worry about them behind me. The line can wait. This is summertime, Hugh. I'm just getting started. Now you best not be throwing it on there all random-like, you dig? I got a system, see? Lettuce, tomatoes, coleslaw, burger, cheese, avocados, burger, cheese, fried egg, bun. Except don't go putting that bun on top just yet—I gotta get my condiments on there too, understand? And make sure that egg ain't too runny, all right? I can't stand eating a soggy burger, you feel me?"

Slim paused for a moment, watching closely as The Beast prepared.

Slim's two patties sizzled on the griddle, right next to a heap of golden-brown onions splashed with olive oil.

"Those onions look mighty fine, yes indeed," Slim continued. "But I ain't going for that today—can't put onions on everything now can you? Now what condiments you got? I know you got ketchup, I can see it all up on your apron. And mustard it looks like, too. Is that

Dijon? I bet it is. But I don't mess around with mustard. No sir. Not on a burger at least. Now here's the real question, Wilt the Stilt: you got any hot sauce my man?"

"All we have is Texas Pete . . ."

Slim slapped his leg like a grandfather. "TEXAS MOTHER FUCKING PETE!"

Slim stuck out his hand to pound fists. The Beast reciprocated with an amused look in his eyes.

"Well *goddamnit* Hugh. You just made my day, you know that? You know that's the *only* hot sauce that I can abide? Out of all the hot sauces in the whole wide world, you've only got Texas motherfucking Pete! Ain't got no sriracha or that Cholula stuff do you? Well shit, Hugh, we may just end up being friends after all. Now I'm gonna be back here quite a bit this summer, so you better get used to it. I like this place, can hear the choir singing. Makes me feel at ease, you dig? I don't cook too often and let's just say this is kind of *my area*. Now why in the hell is this place called The Skillet? Isn't that a griddle you're cooking on? Is your boss illiterate or something? I hope not. No disrespect Hugh, but don't go fucking up my burger now . . . 'cause lord knows you don't wanna mess up Slim's Famous Burger, and I ain't even religious."

Slim ate his burger at the counter without putting it down. Stomach satisfied, he took great pleasure in watching The Beast cook. The two occasionally exchanged niceties but weren't uncomfortable with the silence—at least this is what Sgt. Dykes surmised from his pickup truck. And even though Slim and The Beast weren't more than three feet away from each other, they never felt it necessary to force conversation. From behind a pair of binoculars, Dykes wondered why. When Slim was done he paid the bill and thanked Hugh for his time. The Beast finished his shift and returned to his apartment, a barren place with a single picture of his departed parents (kitchen fire) hanging on the wall. On the other side of town, Slim sunk into a leather couch. He watched a few of The Beast's highlights on YouTube, might have heard someone outside, someone scratching, but when he went out to look there was no one on the street, only the dull hum of a car engine a few houses down. One hour later, down I-40, Sgt. Dykes pulled into a dusty driveway behind my bar. Despite the closed sign, Dykes knocked and knocked again. After waiting for a few minutes like a lost puppy dog, he abandoned his efforts and returned to his cabin, high-stepping through thick brambles to enter a home filled with mold.

5

There are few things more telling than a weak handshake. I knew he'd be trouble by the way he approached the bar, gliding over in some sort of rush. It was summer of 2009.

"Hello. My name is Sergeant Chandler Dykes. But you can call me Dykes. That's what my friends call me. And what about you? You're the bartender, right? Was that your wife I saw the other day? Aren't you going to introduce her to me?"

He was overconfident, like he was hiding something. His body odor was fierce.

"I bet you're Lockart. That's your name, right? Got the place for cheap I bet. That's what I did with my cabin, just out back in the forest. You can see it from your backyard. Well, nice to meet you neighbor!"

His arms were limp. They dangled. He had a terse mouth and squinting eyes. An awkward posture, too. Tense shoulders, all bunched up and caved in. A submissive, squirrelly demeanor. His eyes were always darting, seeking eye contact and conversation. When I first met him he seemed pathetic, a sore loser with a taste for cheap whiskey and self-pity. Those first weeks he was preoccupied, hunched over his laptop. I was lucky he didn't sit at the bar in the beginning. He sat at a table in the corner, a wooden booth just below a framed print of Edward Hopper's *Nighthawks*. He'd sit in front of his black Dell computer—one of those old bulky things with a squishy red pimple on the keyboard—and take advantage of the free Internet or listen to Lord knows what on an outdated MP3 player with those headphones that curl around the back of the ear. But after three weeks of mostly drunken silence, save the slapping on the keyboard and the occasional grunt or moan, Dykes started to sit at the bar. In the beginning he hugged his computer bag close to his chest, but as the whiskeys continued he stored it under the tall stool. Sometimes he reached down and heaved it onto the bar, showing me god-awful CNN headlines, inane Facebook posts, and the like. Thankfully the computer would wheeze and overheat quickly. I never was one for fancy technology in a bar. And so he'd retell his life story—like a lonely geriatric, he seemed to think the past was more real than the future. His complaint-filled soliloquies were laced with many anecdotes and half-truths, but what I remember most is the first time he asked about Slim and The Beast.

He had on a ketchup-stained shirt and there was a foul stench on his breath. His right hand was burned and I caught a whiff of gasoline. It smelled like he'd been standing next to a fire.

"Just got back from Stoke Ridge," Dykes said. "Saw an old friend. Did some house work with him."

"Is that right? Well I've got this door hinge I'd like—"

"Oh, it's a sad town now. Good memories, though. They can

take everything else . . . but they can't take memories, can they! Hey, Lockart . . ." Dykes surveyed his burnt hand. "Can you give me a damp rag? Damn matches. Should've used a lighter, almost let him get away . . . say, you ever heard of this basketball player they call The Beast? Apparently he's a big deal—best player at UNC."

Dykes was worried, he told me. He said his friend was in trouble. I didn't ask 'cause I didn't want to and said I'd never heard of The Beast. "Maybe you should look his real name up."

Dykes grabbed at his backpack and pulled out his computer. "I already have. It's all bullshit. Just anecdotes. See?"

He shoved the laptop onto the bar to show me the Wikipedia page.

"Here, look at this. See? Nothing special. Just stats and facts, that's all."

"Isn't that the point? He's still a college athlete."

"But that's just it. There's got to be more than this, right? I mean this is the Internet—you can find everything. I mean, why is there so little about his parents dying in their kitchen?"

"What do you expect them to say? Sounds like a tragedy in my opinion. But you know how I feel about that laptop on my bar. Please Chandler, I'm going to end up spilling something on that thing. Take it back to your table in the corner. You can plug it in next to the jukebox. You know I don't like gadgets around when I serve drinks."

"Don't worry. It's protected. I mean I can protect it. It's fine. But you're right. I'll go to my table. That's where I belong, right?"

He came in every day at one p.m. and stayed until closing. The image I had of Sgt. Chandler Dykes during the summer and the fall was of a strange, drunken man punching away with two index fingers on a keyboard, occasionally cursing my slow Wi-Fi, drinking enough whiskey to put most men in a coma.

"There's nothing about him!" he said one day during the winter. "Nothing at all! It's all boring sports stuff. Who is this faggot anyway? What is he hiding?"

"What got it into your head that he's hiding something?" I asked. "He's a basketball player, isn't he? What'd you expect? They're not going to tell you his whole life story, even if it is the Internet."

"Well they should. That's the point, right? I mean, there's something more about him . . . I know there's more. There has to be. Why does Slim like—what a faggot. There's more. There's gotta be something . . ."

"Well," I said, "you've been on that thing for months. Maybe you should take a break. Give it some time. Like my wife says, there's more to a man than a website."

"What do you mean?"

"Well, using the Internet to learn about a person is like . . . it's like going to Applebee's for a steak."

"But I love Applebee's."

"That's fine. Lot's of people do. The point is, what you're getting isn't the real thing."

"What do you mean the real thing? It's real. It's steak."

"Well it's frozen. It's industrial. It's not natural, that's all."

"But I go there after Denny's. Grand Slam at Denny's and then Applebee's for a drink."

I chose not to say anything. Whether it was on his barstool or at that wooden table beneath the painting in the corner, Dykes huddled over the digital ether, enveloped by the blue screen, trying to know everything there was to know about The Beast.

"Ah, here we go. This about sums it up, Lockart. Listen to this, here it is: Hugh Dawton-Fields was projected to be the number one pick in the NBA Draft until he knocked out UNC Assistant Coach

Jim Brees. Although it was a year ago, many analysts believe it will affect his draft position."

This wasn't anything new. Dykes was reading from Wikipedia again: 1. High School; 2. College; 3. Family Tragedy and Coach Jim Brees. Other blogs and sports sites highlighted The Beast's supposed aggression, of course, sparking debates over how safe he was for the NCAA, if new rules should be made, if Jim Brees deserved it and why, and what the limits of violence in sports were, et cetera et cetera. All of the analysts speculated, which is all they could do 'cause The Beast never agreed to speak. I had nothing to say 'cause I don't watch television. Like I told Dykes, I rely on conversation for information.

Dykes took this anecdote to heart. "Nothing good can come of it. What kind of person is invisible online? And who goes by *The Beast* anyway? He's dangerous. He should be banned. What if he hurts him?"

"Hurts who?"

"Never mind. But his parents died in a fire . . . you know it's almost impossible for an arsonist to get caught? Forty-eight hours. That's all."

I didn't care for specifics. "Well I'm closing now, Chandler. You can't be staying as late as you did last night."

Like a child, Dykes pretended not to hear me. He continued jabbing at the keyboard with his two pointer fingers.

I asked him to leave a second time.

"Just a couple more seconds. You're going to like this. Trust me."

I asked Chandler a third time: "Chandler, please. I've got to close up now. My wife's waiting for me."

"Two more minutes, Lockart! I'm just Facebook Chatting an old friend from Stoke Ridge."

After thirty minutes Dykes was still there, jabbing away. Thankfully, I had to hand-wash the dishes. I walked around to where he was sitting and picked up his backpack. If he continued to sit there, I said, I'd ban him for the rest of the week.

"Fine. But they're making a documentary about him," Dykes said. "I just found out about it. His life story. You know about Jim Brees? There's a preview on ESPN tomorrow. Too bad you don't have a TV. Maybe we can get it streaming? I'll come in early so we can see . . . See you in the a.m." Dykes gathered his things.

"You're not coming in early, Chandler. I won't be here."

"Geez, okay. I'm leaving. Can I have some peanuts for Larry?"

"Not tonight, Chandler. I don't have any."

He sulked as he walked out, making a point to sigh heavily. He didn't notice the stairs on the front porch and walked right off the edge, falling flat on his face. But he wasn't fazed by his twisted ankle or scraped knees: he frantically pulled out his laptop and examined it for scratches, stroking the case like a cat, finally zipping up the backpack, and patting it like a baby. "Don't worry," he told the computer. "You're fine. You're okay."

I watched Dykes limp away and went around the bar to make sure he didn't come back. As he approached his cabin, high stepping and stomping, stumbling over brambles, swinging his keys around his index finger, he stumbled into a tree. The keys must have fallen somewhere on the forest floor. After a few minutes of drunken stumbling, Dykes pulled out his computer and got down on both knees. The laptop's blue glow illuminated the scene: a lonely drunkard sifting through small twigs and dead leaves.

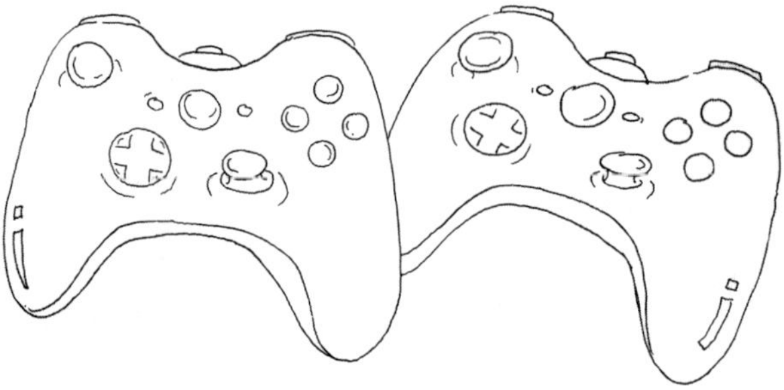

6

The rest of the 2009 academic year was a blur, with ACC basketball, senior parties, and graduation looming. There's nothing like brotherhood or obsession to pass the time. Sergeant Dykes drank more frequently in his rusted pickup on Rosemary Street, surveying The Skillet, Slim, and The Beast. He preferred to watch from the rearview mirror, maybe 'cause he was scared of The Beast, or maybe 'cause of the restraining order, or maybe 'cause he had a plan. Slim had no idea Dykes was following him, and it would take more than a brown pickup idling down the street to signal a warning. For the first time since Stoke Ridge, Slim didn't squirm when he shaved his neck; the scar was a memory now, in the past but not forgotten. And then there was Hugh, who wouldn't have recognized Dykes even if he'd served him, which he did exactly once during 2009. It was on a day when Dykes knew Slim was at the doctor's—a therapy session, in fact, the last Slim would ever attend—that Dykes exchanged niceties with The

Beast. He ordered Slim's Famous Burger, making a point to spit it out and ask for a refund. If The Beast wanted to taste *a real burger*, Dykes said, he should come out to a place called Lockart's Bar. There weren't any coeds there, but it beat the hell out of a shitty food truck. Both intrigued and offended, The Beast made a mental note and gave Dykes a refund without thinking twice.

Toward the end of that peaceful summer, filled with Xbox nights and Sunday brunches, after a few hurricanes had battered the coast but never strayed inland, The Beast received a letter outlining his future:

August 15, 2009

Dear Mr. Hugh Dawton-Fields:

After careful deliberation and discussion with Mr. Jim Brees, the administration has agreed to reinstate you on the Varsity Basketball Team. If you choose to return to the team, you must publicly apologize, on camera, to the University of North Carolina and Mr. Brees.

If you do not intend to return, you will be expelled from the University of North Carolina, effective immediately. Furthermore, Mr. Brees will pursue criminal charges as well as monetary compensation for physical and psychological injuries sustained, effectively replacing the agreement decided upon at your sentencing.

Please inform of us of your decision by the end of this week.

Sincerely,

Adolf McGuirk, Athletic Director

The University of North Carolina

To no one's surprise, the powers-that-be realized how important The Beast was to UNC's championship dreams. Facing a major decline in ticket sales, TV ratings, and merchandising, UNC was desperate to reinstate their breadwinner. Though The Beast knew he had more bargaining power than the letter stipulated, as a student athlete he was in no real position to stand up to the mighty pen-wielders. The choice was simple 'cause he wanted a degree. And while he hated the thought of sitting next to Coach Brees for another year, it gave The Beast more incentive not to foul out at the end of games. He agreed to the reinstatement conditions and followed the proviso letter to a T, getting Slim to take a picture of him holding up a note card that said: "I'm Sorry, University of North Carolina and Mr. Jim Brees." He opened a Twitter account (@TheRemorsefulBeast) and posted the photo for everyone to see. Although they were peeved, Jim Brees and UNC's lawyers were either too lazy or too dumb to reject the apology. What with a *SLAM Magazine* article entitled "2009–2010: The Return of The Beast" (the phrase was printed on countless UNC apparel before the season), no one in the administration nor the athletic department cared enough about semantics to see millions of dollars go by the wayside. They didn't doubt for a second that The Beast wasn't sorry, but they also knew he could win them an ACC championship (the Duke Blue Devils, UNC's nemesis, had graduated their best players the previous year). So even if the administration couldn't get The Beast to apologize on TV, well they could assure the Chapel Hill community that he understood what he'd done and that he was deeply sorry for hitting Jim Brees. They asked The Beast to tweet and re-tweet various apologies, but to this day there remains a single post @TheRemorsefulBeast.

Thousands of Carolina blue "Return of The Beast" and "Fear The Beast" T-shirts covered the backs of giddy kids moving into the dorms. Plastic cups held in storage boxes were returned to Dean Dome vendors; baseball caps and wall posters were back-ordered immediately. In addition to all the money pouring into UNC, marketing executives at video game companies, fast-food restaurants, and sports stores began to brainstorm how exactly to sell The Beast once he made it to the NBA. The draft was fast approaching—June 2010—and the faster they could woo The Beast with promises of untold riches, the better their fiscal projections for the following year. But he never accepted presents and refused to speak with the media. The less he spoke about basketball, the bigger his legend became. And so as new students moved in to the dorms, lugging extra fans and AC units up concrete stairs, East and West Franklin Street started to teem with chatter. *This* was the year UNC would win the ACC Championship; *this* was the year Duke would fall to UNC. The analysts analyzed and the pundits opined. Opponents devised game plans; their fans prepared vicious chants. Yet The Beast didn't falter under the pressure, he saved his energy. When you're winning by twenty points, the best players can take a seat. As the season began, fans booed at his lack of playing time 'cause coaches were saving him for conference play. The Beast loved basketball, there's no question about that. But he didn't live to play, and truth be told, he was happy to take a seat.

To kick off senior year, Slim and The Beast moved into a one-story house in Davie Circle, just off East Franklin Street. Slim had been living down in Carrboro, but his one-bedroom place wasn't big enough for two man-children well over six feet. The house—raised on stilts 'cause it used to flood during hurricane season—was in a modest neighborhood of one-story homes, a short walk away from the Sunrise Biscuit Kitchen, that steamy one-room restaurant serving the best homemade buttermilk biscuits North Carolina has to offer (scrambled egg, Tabasco-spiced sausage, and melted cheddar cheese). Though they

only lived in Davie Circle from August until June, it might as well
have been an entire childhood for all the joy and growth involved.
They ate oatmeal with bananas and brown sugar in the morning.
They argued about dishes 'cause Slim was lazy about the wash. They
scheduled the same times for class so they could walk together up to
campus. They ate lunch at the same time and when they went out
for drinks they always ended the night at Cosmic Cantina, a rustic
Mexican restaurant with a nondescript decor, fresh ingredients, and
burritos bigger than most faces. Slim and The Beast always took
Saturdays off except when The Beast had to play games; otherwise,
the two philosophized and played video games and drank whiskey
and occasionally smoked weed. They hated Greek life and preferred
throwing intimate house parties. Even if they were popular, they kept
to themselves most of senior year. When they came back late in the
a.m. they plopped down on the couch and fell asleep to Seinfeld
reruns and sports documentaries. They often ate at Elmo's Diner on
Sundays, where they preferred tables to booths on account of the
leg space. There was a bond there, you could feel it. They seemed
like brothers. See, The Beast couldn't go anywhere without signing
his nickname, and some students still berated Slim for his time in
Iraq. A few journalists from Stoke Ridge wouldn't seem to go away,
forever stoking rumors about the unpatriotic war veteran who'd turned
to drugs. The Beast was known as the NBA-bound phenom with a
violent streak, while Slim was seen as intimidating proof that nothing
good had come out of Iraq. When they were together, though, people
let them be. Although their public masks were as prominent as ever,
everything that mattered happened inwardly. As leaves started to fall
and the electricity bill decreased, Slim and The Beast settled into senior
year. They did the college thing, of course—occasional hookups and
partying—but both knew the truth about social status and popularity.

During the week Slim studied philosophy while The Beast recalled family recipes—most of the family cookbooks were lost in the fire and The Beast was determined to preserve their memory. Able to sit in the same room for hours in silence—solidarity in solitude, as it came to be called—Slim and The Beast stopped worrying about what others thought and began to question what they thought about themselves. From the outsider's perspective, senior year was a journalistic fiasco: what with talk of the Jim Brees Incident and the Iraq War lingering on, the media thrived on The Beast's secrecy and Slim's unwillingness to respond. But while hundreds of thousands believed "#BeastSighting" was important, in that small house on Davie Circle, Slim and The Beast chose serenity over noise, blocking out everything including the purr of Sgt. Dykes's pickup just down the street.

By March 2010 the NCAA tournament was looming, yet sports fans were already forgetting about The Beast's time at UNC. NBA scouts flocked to the Dean Dome in hopes of wooing their biggest prospect, even if there was some doubt about his talent ceiling. He was a top prospect due to his size rather than a true passion for the game, a realization that soon became obvious during pre-draft workouts. He lost some of his work ethic senior year and often showed up late for morning practices 'cause he'd been down at the local market buying the freshest ingredients. Twice in February he showed up late before a home game to cover a shift down at The Skillet. Now sure, The Beast had a beautiful hook shot and could post-up any man in the nation, but for the life of him he couldn't make it down the court in less than ten seconds. According to a video analysis Dykes played at the bar, "his defense won't cut it in the NBA because he'll have to come out to the three-point line and get around picks. In his first three years as the sole defender on fast breaks, he broke fifteen noses, four wrists, and one player's hand. So even though most opponents can only pray for an ejection, it's only because they don't have the strength to compete." Still, The Beast was a force to be reckoned with, even at the next level of the game. "He may be a ruthless specimen of pure muscle that doesn't play defense," a Boston Celtic said, "but his intimidation factor is undeniable. Bottom line? I know some players who'd refuse to face him. He's the most exciting and terrifying player I've ever seen." Another scout from the Chicago Bulls: "That man is something special. Good for the NBA? I don't know. But he sure is a specimen. He's smart. You see his GPA? The passion will come. He's still young. He's already an All-Star on the stat sheet." Not everyone, however, was so enthralled. "You mean Dawton-Fields?" an anonymous Spurs player remarked, "He's a lunatic. Plain and simple. I can only speak for myself, but I don't want him in the league. This isn't a boxing ring. Fundamentals are important. And I'll say it right now: if he's on the court, I'm not playing. It's not worth it for me. I'm too old for that. I've already won championships. I don't need to get bruised up playing against a guy like him. I don't play that kind of basketball . . . leave it in the streets." A high school teammate-turned-NBA-referee also warned, "Hell no, I never played against him . . . not even in practice. Why? 'Cause he's dangerous. Is letting a wolf into a dog park a good idea? Is releasing a giant hawk above a preschool your idea of fun?"

Whichever way you looked at it, The Beast was a lottery-pick. In a draft that was lacking, he was guaranteed to bring in money. Despite limited minutes (about twenty-five per game) The Beast averaged twenty-seven points and thirteen rebounds per game, sweeping through most teams with terrifying force. March 6, 2010, provided a fitting end to the regular season. Following UNC's dominating run through the ACC, the stage was set for the greatest rivalry in competitive sports, two shades of blue that make all the difference: Duke-UNC, the battle of Tobacco Road, nine miles apart down Highway 15-501. Back in those days when regional differences were respected, before greed trumped tradition, when rivalry trumped money, history was something to be honored and respected, not a commodity to be sold on account of football season. And so the stage was set for the 2010 ACC Tournament Final, remembered as one of the greatest and most stomach-turning examples of competition ever seen on a basketball court.

The game started out normally enough. Duke was shooting lights out from three, picking apart UNC's 3-2 zone defense. The Beast made up for it though, garnering fifteen points, ten rebounds, seven blocks, and only three fouls by the end of the first half. Halfway through the second half it was clear neither team was giving in: The Beast was playing his smartest game since the beginning of the season, avoiding foul trouble by blocking shooters' views with his pan hands, yet Duke was still shooting a season-high 55 percent from three. Slim gleefully cheered for Duke from behind UNC's bench. The coaching staff hated that Slim sat directly behind 'em but couldn't do or say anything 'cause he had season tickets (Jim Brees, in fact, received a one-game suspension that season for turning around and threatening to slap Slim in the face). As Duke continued to put it in the basket, UNC's wrinkled fans could only shake their bejeweled heads in vain. But with eight minutes left, UNC made a furious comeback, going on a 25-10 run to all but secure the ACC championship. With one minute to go, UNC was up by eleven. Everyone except Duke fans thought the game was sealed. Slim continued to cheer 'cause he knew Duke had a chance if The Beast wasn't on the bench. Slim knew his friend would be fouled, and he knew there was a chance he'd react. Normally he would've hated to see his friend lose his temper, but this was Duke-UNC—sometimes even family comes second to the rivalry.

The band section in the Dean Dome started playing, "We Are The Champions." More than a few Carolina fans left the stadium to beat the traffic. As the Dean Dome grew silent, many tried to turn back; but when they realized what was happening, it was already too late. A barrage of Duke three-pointers and several UNC turnovers cut the lead in half—from eleven points down to five in a matter of seconds. After UNC missed a crucial free throw, Duke ran up the court and didn't hesitate to hit another three. Now UNC was only up by two. They took the ball out at the far end of the court, under their own basket. The pompom girls couldn't help but cheer nervously. Their tight-panted male counterparts stopped doing front flips and fancy cartwheels. Hoping for a turnover and another missed free throw, Duke called on a benchwarmer by the name of Michael Jinson to put UNC's worst free-throw shooter on the foul line. But Michael "Jincy" Jinson never should've been on the basketball court. He was a six-foot-one freshman with a mop of floppy hair. Before that night he'd never said hello to a man over seven feet. Although Jincy was a great defender willing to sacrifice his body for the play, he was nothing more than the prototypical Duke benchwarmer, out there to scrap, follow orders, and take a charge. So when one of Jinson's teammates sarcastically said, "You won't be able to take a charge on The Beast. The only way to get him ejected is to get your finger up his ass," well, the young go-getter took it literally, considering it his duty to sacrifice his index finger for the game. And so he shuffled out into the spotlight, a ceremonial sacrifice. The Beast had seen this tactic plenty of times before: late-game substitutions to put him on the free-throw line (he wasn't a terrible shooter, but still a weak one at 65 percent). He was already frustrated, but he tried to keep his composure—he'd been elbowed in the gut countless times and in the final minute he took an "accidental" palm to the face. So when he saw Michael Jinson checking in at the sidelines, The Beast was ready. He knew he'd get fouled if he caught the basketball, but since he was taking the ball out of bounds he figured he could avoid being part of the play. And so The Beast took a deep breath and shook his head at Michael Jinson as he made his way onto the court.

The Beast inbounded the ball under the basket. UNC's point guard tripped and bonked the ball straight back to him. By the time The Beast reached down, Jincy's finger was already on its way. Only one cameraman saw it. Everyone else focused on the ball. Michael Jinson screeched and wailed on the floor. The audience gasped. There was a collective scream. Sucking in air, chest heaving up and down, Jinson whimpered like a child as he clutched his right hand, his fingers twisted and bleeding, gushing onto the court. The *New York Times* called it "one of the most grotesque injuries seen in sports." At least one UNC fan vomited into a 64-ounce cup. The Beast, in a rage, was held back until the replay confirmed everyone's suspicions. Sure, Jinson's hand went up The Beast's shorts, but did this warrant The Beast crushing it? He was escorted off the court. Once the ball boys mopped the last bloodstains with crimson towels, Duke made two free throws and gained possession to win the game on a buzzer-beater, though no one cared about the score.

The Beast was banned from the NCAA tournament, effectively ending his college career. And although Duke won the 2010 National Championship, all the talk in college basketball was about The Foul Heard Around the World. In the months leading up to the NBA Draft, it seemed basketball fans were split on The Beast's antics. On the one hand they were terrified of what he'd do next, but on the other this was part of why they watched sports. "Wait 'til he gets here," an anonymous OKC Thunder player said, "We'll show him what a hard foul *really means*. No, I'm not scared of him. Of course not! He

won't score a single basket. You can quote me on that." In the words
of a radio host: "Well yes, of course Larry, you're right. He can be
brutish at times. But I saw the replay. Do you know *why* he attacked
that kid Jinson? These kids are still kids. You've got to remember
that. Do you know about his past? Tragic story, really." Whatever the
opinion (and there were plenty), The Beast was a guaranteed top-ten
pick. And so he packed his car—a rickety '93 Jeep Cherokee with a
massive stick shift—and hung a pair of furry red dice on his rear-view
mirror. He only needed a UNC bumper sticker to remember his college
years 'cause he had the diploma and his best friend in the car. The
windshield wipers had no lubrication and screeched back and forth
to remove drops of bird shit. The passenger side-mirror was broken,
too—Slim stuck his head out the window to help check for blind spots.
If their mothers had been around, they would've made a comment
about the lack of airbags. The seatbelts were also useless 'cause they
had no stopping mechanism, the only benefit being they were never
tight around the waistband. The passenger's seat had no stopping
mechanism either; whenever The Beast pulled up to a stoplight the
seat lunged back and forth on the track. If they got into an accident,
Slim would be ejected—the car was flat-out dangerous, but neither
of them thought twice as they drove away from a coming storm.
They didn't have many people to say goodbye to—teammates, a few
professors, and a couple acquaintances—before descending onto I-40,
heading west. It was raining when they left, and you may not know
it if you aren't from around here, but summertime means summer
storms, and not just thunderstorms, but proper hurricanes. And in
June 2010, Hurricane Beverly was welcoming in the season, one of
the earliest category fives in history, churning off the coast, picking up
water and speed. The meteorologists said it'd make landfall the very
night Slim and The Beast left, but they weren't too worried about it

'cause there's nowhere to hide during a hurricane. And even if Beverly was moving around fifty miles per hour (not her wind speed of course, which was up near one-hundred-fifty), well, driving west at seventy-five miles per hour would give 'em plenty of time. But I'm not one for word problems; the bottom line was Slim and The Beast departed the same day Hurricane Beverly arrived. They would make one final stop off Exit 263 at a bar named Lockart's. That's where I come in.

7

They stopped here 'cause of a rumor about the best burger in town. Slim didn't care 'cause he thought The Skillet's was the best this side of the Mississippi, but The Beast recalled a customer spitting out a burger last summer and was eager to taste what he'd heard was the best sandwich around. Neither was particularly hungry, but this wasn't about sustenance so much as it was about pride. And so, less than a mile off Exit 263, after sitting in hurricane traffic for close to an hour, a red Jeep Cherokee pulled up to Lockart's.

My bar was nestled comfortably amongst the trees on a hill above New Hope Creek. It was in a clearing surrounded by tall pines with a dirt parking lot out front, an oasis of levity next to the forest's edge. Wind chimes hung from two small oak trees in the backyard and from an abstract, metallic sculpture that reflected the sunlight, designed and built by Jane, my wife. Lockart's was a hybrid, both a home and a bar: while my wife and I had our own place down near the creek, years ago we both agreed we each needed a place to call our own. There was a stairway out back—steep wooden steps with sizable gaps between 'em—leading up to a small bedroom. The roof was slanted and I had to duck like a kid in his fort. The carpet was white. I slept on a futon next to a small blue light. As for the bar itself, well, there wasn't much inside; but just 'cause something's empty doesn't mean it's deserted. The jingling of the bell and creaking of the screen door exposed a long corridor leading to the backyard. There were no framed pictures along the corridor walls. Upon entering through the screen door, immediately to the right a doorless portal lead into the tavern, whose three rectangular windows beckoned in the eastern sun. The framed print of *Nighthawks* was directly across the room, on the wall above a jukebox that doesn't work anymore. Four tall stools lined up in front of the bar on the left, high enough that short legs couldn't reach the floor. The bar was thick, dark oak. It ran half the length of the tavern, with a hatch at the far right end that was heavy to lift. In the other corner was a door leading to the kitchen. There were three booths next to the windows—thick wooden tables, also dark oak with a waxy finish on top, which Dykes liked to scrape at with his unkempt fingernails—but most people sat at the bar 'cause Lockart's wasn't a restaurant at the time. The truth was there was no burger, at least not one I shared with the public, and even if there was a kitchen, I'd only cooked in it once (the ceiling's wooden beams made me wary of kitchen fires). It was down the corridor to the right, directly behind the bar, but I installed a door in the corner so I could easily access the kitchen. It had a window looking out on the backyard and a small door that led to a screened-in porch. The whole place smelled like incense—Nag Champa, to be precise—'cause my wife and I don't like the smell of beer-stained floors and Clorox.

I might've mentioned the screen door was rusty. The hinges creaked when The Beast came in. A breeze rushed in along with a mosquito. It was a thick, humid day, on account of the coming storm. Heavy clouds descended on the landscape and muffled the sun, but for the moment they still accompanied the turquoise blue above. Cicadas chirped and bees buzzed, but the deer weren't ones for alliteration. They were out there of course, hiding in the forest with other creatures, much wiser than insects when it comes to forecasting storms. Slim blasted in just behind The Beast, knocking loose a door hinge that fell to the ground and rolled across the wooden floor. The bell above the door jingled, stating their presence. A gust of muggy air swept in as the two sat down at the bar.

Slim asked for a whiskey and when he could order a burger. They were in a rush, he said. This man was headed to the NBA.

The sun crept through the blinds, illuminating the bar with natural light. The air was thick with cigarette smoke.

"Excuse me," Slim repeated. "Anyone back there? *I said I'll have a whiskey*. And my man over here will have an iced tea. What kind of a business is this? Maybe they're in the kitchen . . ."

Slim stood up, put his hands on the bar, and looked behind the bar as if he were verifying something. "Now listen up, whoever's back there. I know you're there 'cause the door ain't closed. You know who this man is? They call him The Beast."

"He's probably just in the bathroom, Slim," The Beast said without a hint of irritation.

"Someone's messing with us, Hugh. I can feel it."

I let out a smoke-filled sigh from the corner table where I'd watched 'em come in. "No use getting antsy, mister," I said. "This place isn't known for burgers. I'm the owner, see? And I don't serve alcohol between the hours of two and three. That's just policy. It isn't anything against you boys, but you'll have to wait for that whiskey." I walked over to the two of 'em. "The name's Lockart. Welcome to my bar." Something about Slim's eyes seemed familiar.

Sunlight reflected off of the tiny dust particles floating around the bar. The Beast squinted and held out his hand. "Excuse me sir, nice to meet you. Do you think we could have a drink? We're not staying long, what with the hurricane. Just a quick pit stop, that's all. Trying to beat the traffic."

I shook his hand. The Beast continued: "We don't want any trouble, just a drink and a burger, if possible. We've heard a lot about it—one of the best in the area, so we're told. And a whiskey and a lemonade."

"Sweet tea."

"What?"

"Sweet tea," I said. "You didn't order lemonade. Your friend there asked for a whiskey and a sweet tea."

"Sweet tea, right."

"You got a problem with that?" Slim threatened.

"Well," I took a long drag from my cigarette as I went around the bar, "I guess I do, don't I? Like I said before, I don't serve alcohol between two and three. Now, I'd be more than happy to get you some sweet tea or lemonade. As for the burgers, well this is a bar. You may have heard a rumor or two, but that's just human tendency. Matter of fact, there's a man I can't quite figure out who's been coming in here blabbering about his nephew and a burger joint for a while now. I could make an exception for the burger, depending on the company. But as for the whiskey? I'm sorry, not until the clock hits three."

I extinguished my cigarette on the countertop. "Now I don't know if you noticed when you first came in, Slim—"

"How do you know my name? I didn't introduce myself."

"And it was quite rude of you too, if I may say so myself. When it comes to names, I pay attention. Your friend here said it about fifteen seconds ago. As for you," I looked at Hugh, "So they call you The Beast?"

"People call me that—"

"He's famous," Slim interrupted. "You don't watch UNC basketball?"

"Can't say I do. I stopped a while back. Nice to make your acquaintance. Now as I was saying, *Slim*, I don't know if you noticed when you first came in, but you dislodged a door hinge and now it's on the floor." I pointed down. "I just spent the last five hours down on my knees trying to fix it. But apparently I didn't do too good a job. My wife does the real work around here . . . she's a whiz with that kind of stuff. Screws and hinges aren't my specialty—for the life of me I can't figure those kinds of things out. Did you see the sculptures out front? Jane, my wife, said I needed to add some panache. She's been telling me to put that painting up for weeks. Now you mentioned you're in a hurry, but you can't outrun a hurricane. As for your nickname, well, I've heard of you, and I've also heard of The Skillet. See, this guy's been coming in here—somewhat of a nut—talking about you and burgers all day long. His nephew, too. Always carries a Polaroid. Searching the Internet for something . . . can't seem to figure you out."

"What's there to figure out?"

"That's what I'd like to know. But this *is* something. I mean what are the odds? Some guy's been blabbering on and on about a kid named The Beast for nearly a year, and then suddenly here you are! So tell me, what *are* you doing in my bar? You know you're driving straight into a storm?"

"We're not driving into it, we're getting out," Slim replied.

"Not tonight you aren't," I chuckled. "All this technology and you forget to use your eyes. You don't need a satellite to see the whole interstate is clogged. The storm's acomin'. No use trying to escape it. But this is interesting, take a seat. It's almost time to serve the whiskey."

"I thought you said you didn't serve until three p.m.," Slim said.

"Well I don't. We've got ten minutes. But you can start with water."

Slim looked at The Beast. The Beast looked at his watch. "I think we need to get going. Like you said, there's traffic to beat."

"Ha," I smiled. "Did I say that? Sometimes you beat the traffic, and sometimes the traffic beats you. So do me the courtesy and wait a couple minutes. Tell me about yourselves . . . I've been hearing about you for over a year now . . . don't I deserve the chance to hear it from the source?"

Slim and The Beast shifted in their seats, trying to catch each other's eye. They were giving each other the look young people do when they're trying to get away, formulating an escape plan as an elder starts to ramble.

"You want to leave, I get it. Okay, that's fine. But at least wait for me to serve you one glass of whiskey."

The Beast was polite. "One whiskey, all right. We can wait for one drink, Slim. So why the three o'clock rule?"

"Well it's simple, really. I used to have what some might call a drinking problem. Between the hours of two and three I don't touch the stuff at all. Everyone needs limits, no matter how far gone. So I lock up the booze in that cabinet up above—right up on that dusty shelf with the plated glass case?—and drink as much water as my bladder can handle until three o'clock comes around. Now, it's not like I'm scrambling for the stuff when the clock hits three. Sometimes I'll go for days before drinking again. Like yesterday and today when I was trying to fix that door hinge. But *the point*, the bottom line, is setting limits. This Dykes character who keeps coming in could learn a thing or two about that . . ."

Slim choked on his water. "What'd you call him?"

"Dykes. Chandler Dykes, though he likes to be called Sergeant. The bozo's been coming in here for over a year now. He just goes on and on. You'd think this nephew of his had died or something. But I think he's just lonely, that's all."

Slim took a deep breath and stood up. "Hugh, let's get out of here."

I was confused. "Hey! Wait a minute now."

"Slim, what's the problem?" The Beast asked.

Slim made for the door and then stopped at the threshold. After a moment he looked back up. "You said he lives around here?"

"Who, Dykes?" I asked. "Yes indeed, just out back behind the bar in that rickety old cabin . . ."

Slim continued to shake his head. "Who's this nephew he's been talking about? You said he has a Polaroid? Chandler Dykes doesn't have a sister or a brother . . ."

"Some kid with a fishing net standing in a creek . . . what, you know the man?"

"Hugh, let's go. I'll tell you in the car."

"Now hold up just one second," I said. "I deserve some kind of explanation, too. I was kind enough to let you into my bar . . ."

Slim's voice was stern. "It's a long story, Mr. Lockart. Let's just say Dykes and I don't get along. Hugh, come on man. It's time to head out."

The Beast was confused but still stood up to leave.

"Well for what it's worth, he told me he's heading to Milwaukee," I said. "Something about starting a new life. He found his nephew up there."

Slim turned around. "Hugh, he's following us . . ."

"What the hell are you talking about Slim?"

"We gotta get out, now."

"Wait a minute!" I exclaimed. "That's where I've seen you! You're the kid in the Polaroid, aren't you! That explains a lot. You went to Stoke Ridge Military Academy? Fought in Iraq and got dishonorably discharged? What were you thinking, attacking him at the award ceremony like that?"

Slim became agitated. There was weakness in his eyes. "Me attacking him? What the hell are you talking about?" His breath was short and pronounced.

"Please, sit down. One whiskey, I promise. Come have a seat. It think we've got a lot to talk about."

The lingering sunlight poured into the bar, its golden beam stretching across the front hallway. I poured three whiskeys. They returned to their stools. Slim was anxious. The Beast was intrigued.

"Who the hell is this guy, Slim? And how did he know we're driving up to Milwaukee?" The Beast asked.

"I'll explain later, Hugh. What's he been saying, Lockart?"

"Well, a lot of things," I replied. "More than I care to recount, in fact. He's either at that table in the corner with his laptop looking up your friend here, or he's sitting right where you're sitting, lamenting one thing or another. Mostly he talks about his past, his childhood. And about you, Slim. As for The Beast—now what's your real name again? I hope I don't have to call you The Beast all night . . ."

"Hugh."

"As for you, Hugh, well, he keeps saying you've got a secret, whining about you never giving interviews. He can't seem to figure you out."

"Figure me out? What does that mean?"

Slim's anger returned. "He's stalking you too, now. Fuck this, Hugh. Let's get out."

Slim stood up. I protested. "You think you're going to get far with Hurricane Beverly? They're setting up roadblocks and detours all around. Wherever you go, you're going to have to hunker down. And if you want my guess, he's scared of the storm. I saw him yesterday and he said he wasn't going out. I haven't seen him today, which is rare. Usually he stays from morning until night."

The Beast shook his head. "Slim, what the hell is this all about? If Mr. Lockart is right, we're gonna be stuck. Look outside, the clouds are churning. We might not get far enough—"

"We can make it to Greensboro, even if it takes a couple of hours," Slim replied. "If he's sleeping in he's drunk. He won't follow us. Mr. Lockart can delay him. Right?"

"Call me Lockart."

"You can delay him, Lockart. It's safer than being stuck out here in the boondocks. Hugh, you don't know Dykes. I'm telling you, we've gotta go now."

"But *I know* Dykes," I cut Slim off. "And you know as well as I do he won't stop following you. And good luck finding a room in a motel tonight. You think you two are the only ones trying to get out of town? There are ten thousand people coming inland from the coast. I-40 is jammed all the way to Tennessee. Beverly's the real deal. She isn't messing around. Just this one whiskey. Maybe you'll learn something. Just hear me out."

Slim hung his head at the bar. The Beast waited for his friend's response.

"Look," I said. "I'll be the first to tell you, I know he's a nut—"

"You have no idea."

"Well wait a minute Slim, just hear me out. I know how to calm him. That I can promise you. I don't think he'll do anything if I'm around."

Slim laughed.

"Look," I replied. "If you know Dykes like I know him, you know he's a wacko. But I've learned how to reason with him. I know how to talk to him. So if you stay for a while and tell me your side of it, maybe I can help you out. I'm not making any promises, but he trusts me, that's all. And truth be told, I want to hear your side of the story. And Hugh's, too. Maybe we can all figure Dykes out. Either way, I've got information you need. Of that I can promise you . . ."

As Slim deliberated and The Beast pondered, I continued to talk. "Look. The longer it takes for him to find you, the more extreme his response, right? He isn't a patient man. You know that, Slim. But if he wanted to hurt you he'd have already done it—he's already mentioned watching you . . . I'd venture to guess you lived in Davie Circle?"

"Goddammit."

"Okay, but like I said, he's prepared to make the trek up to Milwaukee. That's where the draft is, isn't it? This doesn't end 'cause you're leaving. You're all he's got. And is that what you want? Dykes constantly following you? I might be able to help you. Maybe you were meant to show up at the bar. In any case, the more you know about him, the easier it'll be to confront him. Whether you confront him here in my bar or in a parking lot in Milwaukee, at least here you'll know what he's been going on and on about. He won't be coming in today, I promise. He's terrified of the storm. Won't leave his house. But you don't need me to tell you that he won't quit—he's been showing me that Polaroid for the better part of a year now. Unless something gives, he'll keep coming, no doubt."

My words struck a nerve. Slim ripped into his index fingernail with his front teeth. He looked out the door and shook his head. "Fuck."

"Slim, tell me what's going on. Let's at least hear Lockart out . . ."

Slim walked over to the window. "I haven't had to think about him in three years. And now he's back, stalking you, too? Talk about shitty luck. That's how it's always been . . . but if he's been coming in for a year, why isn't he here right now, Lockart?"

"I told you, Slim, he's scared of Beverly. In truth I think he's afraid of thunder . . ."

My words reminded Slim of something. The wind rustled the front porch wind chimes. The light was dimming. The air was heavy. The clouds were thickening, darker now.

"Alright, Lockart." Slim sat down. "One whiskey, let's talk."

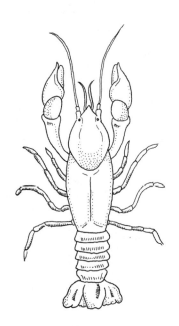

8

Slim was born in an elevated trailer, atop a hill above a creek that runs under the James Taylor Bridge. The place smelled like Hot Pockets, wet laundry, and mold. The crawlspace smelled like somewhere rodents go to die. The trailer was a tube small enough to tow with a pickup, a flimsy metallic structure whose innards were made of crackling drywall. It was neither comfortable nor sturdy, but it was enough to suffice. There was a bedroom, hallway, living room/kitchen (the kind with a cooking island and a two-burner stove), bathroom, short hallway, then Slim's bedroom (which could only fit a single bed). Insulation foam crept out of the plaster walls throughout the year, doing little to keep the air in or out. The roof leaked constantly, as did the kitchen sink; the drip-drip-dripping kept Slim up at night. Whenever he had the courage (he was afraid of the dark as a kid), he'd tiptoe out of his room, down the hallway, and into the living room/kitchen, where his feet would sink into the sodden brown carpet that covered the entirety of this home. He'd squish back through the kitchen on his tiptoes and crawl into bed, his feet poking out of the sheets 'cause it was muggy and hot. The walls in his bedroom were also dark brown and they absorbed most of his trusty nightlight's blue glare. The rest of the tube was filled with exposed, swinging light bulbs whose fuses were almost always out. Sometimes his mother slept in her bedroom, but usually she piled damp laundry on top of her bed and got high in the living room, where she often passed out. The trailer trembled during hurricane season and should've been destroyed; the creek down below often flooded over, but it never reached the trailer on the hilltop. When the torrents came, Slim would sit on the porch outside and watch the rushing water under the elevated home carry leaves and other debris to the bubbling creek below. After Hurricane Fran, a metallic roof was installed, and Slim became something of an insomniac when it rained at night (the metallic patter up above just a louder version of the leaky kitchen sink). Tall swaying pines blocked the sun from Slim's home in the summer, but they also kept the trailer cold in the winter when it needed the heat. Wilhelmina used fans to blow stale air throughout the trailer, which always carried the scent of her moldy laundry and marijuana. Trees showered pine needles in the fall, and icicles slapped the aluminum roofing in the winter. In the springtime the rain poured off the roof and carried dead mice down to the creek. Mid-spring, when the trees turned yellow, pollen and dander floated down. Slim had his fair share of allergies—cats, pollen, dust, and the like—and thanks to his mother's cat Eddy, who shat in a box in the house, he learned to live with pungent smells and itchy, watery eyes. He got used to the stomachaches and the silence and the loneliness, all of these caused by his mother's addiction to marijuana.

Indeed, the oral exhaust of Wilhelmina Jenkins fogged Slim's first impression of this here world. She was a single mother with a grotesque mole on her chin—it sprung a singular coarse black hair that never saw a pair of tweezers in her life. Her long brown hair reached to her calves, and her rather petite body could store obscene amounts of weed smoke. Her favorite activity, regardless of season, was to mow the brown lawn with a joint in her mouth, kicking up brown dirt and small rocks with an outdated lawn mower that didn't have a blade protector and made an antiquated sound. She spent her summers in the yard, white noise blocking everything else out. In the winter she used buckets of boiling water to force the grass out. Long story short, Wilhelmina despised her parents, which is why she was always high— the only time they hugged her was out in public, usually at church. As a kid she acted out 'cause she wanted her parents to care, and as a teenager she acted out 'cause she wanted them to notice. After her father died of a heart attack from drinking too many Red Bull vodkas at a college reunion, her mother moved to Miami and abandoned her eighteen-year-old pregnant daughter with nothing more than a tubelike trailer next to a creek. By the time Slim came screeching into the world, any inkling of a maternal instinct had seeped into the Doritos-stained couch, down in the crevices among the remnants, deep down near the bottom, where useless pennies and stale cookie crumbs hid in the darkness.

Most of Slim's earliest memories were of a burnt tongue, scalding Hot Pockets, and a blaring lawn mower outside. Wilhelmina only hugged him when she wanted to cuddle, so Slim spent most of his infancy sitting on a soggy floor building towers of Lincoln Logs and swallowing more than a few Legos. When the smell of burnt firewood beckoned Wilhelmina back indoors, Slim stayed in his room instead of watching mom get high. In the warm months, though, he found peace in the ankle-deep water of James Taylor Creek. He spent as much time as he could outside, alone with his thoughts.

"I loved searching for crawdads, but could never find the right spot," Slim recounted. I poured him another drink. His edge was slowly melting. He rested his forearms on the bar.

He'd poke at the mud with a stick and splash around in hopes of scaring up the evasive creatures, his jeans rolled up, his voice ready to yelp at the first ripple. He'd stand there for hours, waving off Wilhemina's calls for supper; and when he got hungry enough, he'd trudge up the hill in dirty brown socks. His mother never told him to take the socks off once inside. "Whenever I walked back inside dinner was usually half-eaten, leftovers on the kitchen counter with my mom passed out on the couch, melted cheese dangling from her mouth. I hated being at home, but school was both a blessing and a curse 'cause my momma's second favorite activity—after the lawn mower—was getting high in the car. I tried to stick my head out the window but it didn't really work . . . I usually got hotboxed. I don't know how she never got caught. Anyway, at school let's just say I wasn't treated well. I was put in the special-ed class 'cause I was too high to respond. And kids love making fun of the quiet types. They prescribed me Ritalin, which gave me nausea. I got pissed off, you know? Couldn't make any friends. So by the time I was on fifty milligrams a day, I was missing class to use the bathroom every twenty minutes, which defeated the purpose of focusing in the first place. Forget about thriving. I was terrible at science and math. I liked to talk things out, but no one ever listened. That's why I spent so much time outside."

Slim sipped his whiskey. "I was always down by the creek." He bit his other index fingernail down to its cuticle. He looked out the window and said something to himself.

"Then one day I went downstream, just to take a walk. And that's when I saw them through a clearing. All of 'em had nets. And there was this big, impressive man snapping pictures and giving 'em high fives."

Slim resumed the nail biting. "I'd never seen anything like it. He was like a savior. He was everything I wasn't—tall and strong and confident. And all his cadets were laughing in the creek, picking up buckets full of crawdads, playing with each other like kids are supposed to, right? All those years looking for crawdads, all 'cause I was in the wrong part of the creek. And what was most amazing was that they invited me to play. I felt like part of a tribe that day. First time I'd ever felt part of a group in my life."

Slim almost smiled. "I didn't know anything about the military, but Dykes convinced me. And I wanted to trust him. I had to get out. So the next week he came over to sign the papers. And just like that I was part of Stoke Ridge Military. Momma was so high she took off her shirt on account of the heat. She didn't know what she was signing but she did it just the same. I packed my sports bag, and just like that I was gone."

Slim paused to sip his whiskey.

"He was nice in the beginning. I felt like there was a connection. It was the first time someone ever cared about me, you know? Uncle Chandler, I called him. Uncle Sarge. But that lasted about three weeks. Then he started making me come to his office—in the daytime to do pushups, at night to sleep. He said it was better 'cause the kids would bother me in the dorms. He said as long as I stuck close he'd protect me. So there I was, the new kid, a scrawny thirteen-year-old. But at first I was happy 'cause I trusted him. Soon enough things changed, though, as they always seem to. It was a military academy, plain and simple—they shave your head and tell you obeying is always right. You eat the same thing every day, wake up at the same hour. I was used to being outside, having my freedom to walk around. It started to weigh on me after a couple months. And the more Dykes told me the kids didn't like me, the more I relied on him. The more I felt alone. Sooner or later I realized it wasn't true at all . . . he just wanted me all to himself. He was lonely, too.

"He put me on the JV basketball team right when I got there. Made me spend after-school hours with him for one-on-one practice. He didn't know shit about the game, but all the kids were forced to play 'cause their divorced moms and dads said they needed to learn about team spirit. And Dykes is jealous, you know, so once he saw the camaraderie with the team? That's when he got obsessed with keeping me around. You could see it in his eyes. He'd tickle my stomach before games or squeeze my love handles. I never questioned why he didn't do it to the others. When we lost, he made us do pushups in his office."

"The whole team in his office?" The Beast asked.

"Yeah, it was small. But that just gave him an excuse to tell us to take our shirts off. It was hot and there wasn't a fan. So he'd sit behind his desk that had a stuffed opossum on it, screaming at us until we were exhausted."

"Stuffed opossum?" The Beast asked.

"Pink gums and glaring teeth. It was creepy for sure. Seemed like it was staring at us. But Dykes didn't realize misery loves company. All those late-night workout sessions created a bond. The cadets started to dislike him. Started to act out and like me, too. I became the ringleader when I realized he wasn't worth shit."

Slim sipped his drink. "You can't train kids to kill without giving 'em a reason. And all of us wanted to get back at Dykes. But we held our tongues during workouts, at least for a time. Do you have a bathroom, Lockart? I need to take a piss."

"Just out there in the hall."

Slim returned from the bathroom a few minutes later. "That's his cabin out back? All run down?"

"Sure is," I answered. "In those brambles and bushes. I've only been there once. Don't fancy going back again. It's hard enough to get to . . . that dirt road stops one hundred yards away."

I poured Slim another glass.

"Where was I?" he responded.

"All of you wanted to get back at Dykes."

"Right. The thing was, we were all kind of waiting for puberty. I know I was excited to see how tall I was gonna get. Of course, we were impressionable, and for a time the threat of humiliation damn near worked. We ran until we vomited and did pushups until dawn, supposedly proving our self-worth in hopes of making Dykes proud. We didn't want to be called sissies, you know? Funny how powerful Dykes felt calling us cowards . . . But Dykes picked on me in particular, tried to make me some kind of pariah. He wanted to have me to himself, I think. So he made me look weaker than the others by putting me down, beating me. I don't need to go into details, but I saw more than a few punches. But at the same time he favored me, like abusive boyfriends who buy their girls jewelry."

"How so?" The Beast asked.

"Took me out to dinner. Bought me shoes and clothes and what not. For a time it worked 'cause the other kids got jealous. And since they knew Dykes would defend me, they started to fear me. But I didn't like being feared—it was just like being back at school, but with bigger muscles. In the end it isn't any different though. You end up feeling ostracized regardless. And that was Dykes, of course—he was the most feared man at Stoke Ridge."

"So what changed?" The Beast asked.

"You mean with me or with Dykes? For me, I realized the other

kids didn't fear me so much as they felt sorry. Dykes probably learned
the same thing after eating alone every night. He pretended like it
was 'cause he wanted to, but you can only keep up that kind of
self-righteous image for so long."

"Seclusion will do that . . ." The Beast said.

"Seclusion and alcohol. Dykes was a bona fide drunk. But like I
said, once puberty came around it was a whole different ball game.
I no longer had any reason to fear him. I grew eleven inches junior
year. Five feet seven to six feet five . . . all of a sudden Dykes was
short. His mistake was sticking with my group of cadets instead of
taking on a new group of young'uns. He didn't intimidate us anymore.
He no longer had any power. And you know what happens when
megalomaniacs get scared . . . they put the pressure on. They start
oppressing. That's the only way he could maintain supremacy. Just
take a look at history. So he started abusing me physically. He'd hit
me with a sock full of pennies so the doctor wouldn't notice when I
got physicals. I don't know how many times I had to go late-night to
his office just to get beat up. Always with my shirt off. If I refused,
he'd knock me out on the spot. It was weird though—somehow I was
still attached to him. I know it isn't right, but it's the truth. I couldn't
let go. Stockholm syndrome or some shit. It was all I'd ever known.
So even when he hit me, there was some weird kind of comfort . . ."

"And did he beat the other ones too?"

"Not like he did me. It was different with me . . . there was real
hate there, I think. He broke a rib once. More black eyes than I care
to count. Of course, none of that compares to this here scar." Slim
raised his neck. "But even if I was still skinny, now I had height. And
'cause I knew he didn't understand the difference between leadership
and authority, well, as I got bigger, I got smarter, too. I started to call
him out on his loneliness, asking where his friends were, why he was

always eating dinner alone, that kind of stuff. Making fun of him for watching teenagers do pushups. And then after 9/11 everyone started talking about war, and I knew I'd be on the first transport out. I was easy pickings 'cause I made sure I was the best cadet in the academy. So you better believe, when he realized I was leaving? Dykes lost his shit. I think he envied me. And so the beatings got worse. Somehow he thought that'd keep me around. But by that point, I started to fight back with my fists. The scars got worse, but those were only skin deep. I was nasty with him, I'll admit it. Really personal stuff. But he deserved every word of it. So his scars became deeper, more psychological than mine. And then there was one night . . . well, I don't like being reminded."

The Beast didn't ask any questions. He waited for Slim to talk.

"Fighting a war on the other side of the world started to seem like a mighty fine alternative," Slim resumed. "I was only seventeen, though. I had to wait another year."

"Did anyone know Dykes was beating you?"

"Sure. But you know how that kind of thing goes. It's a culture of violence. General Haith, the director, well, he was a kind man. He promised that he'd talk to some of the higher-ups and see if he couldn't get me fighting in Iraq. Again, I had to get out of there as fast as possible. I wasn't convinced about our reasons for going to Iraq or anything like that, but that just shows you how determined I was to leave. I made a calendar to count the days. General Haith got me out of there fast."

"So it got that bad?"

"I'm not going into details, Hugh, but those last months were brutal. I fought in Fallujah, sure, but that time at Stoke Ridge was the scariest of my life. But there's no use in lamenting the past . . . all that to say, by the time I graduated I was the best goddamn soldier Stoke Ridge had ever seen. I channeled all that bullshit into becoming a warrior. All of that anger I channeled out in Iraq. I'm not proud of it, not particularly. But they didn't stand a chance. I shit you not I could shoot a quarter off a cow's head and throw a grenade a hundred yards. By the time they shipped me out to Fallujah? It all burst out."

Slim's demeanor shifted. He was suddenly more at ease.

"Talk about a crazy idea, right? Letting kids go straight from a military academy to war. But it worked, at least on paper. No amount of training can prepare you for that shit. And you gotta remember: we'd never seen so much as a goddamn gunshot wound, let alone a street scattered with bodies and limbs. People's heads exploding, brains oozing out, seeing your buddies filled with holes like Swiss cheese. The only reason I was there was 'cause of Dykes, really. I blame him in a way for having to figure it all out. But his strategy worked, I guess. We stuck together on the battlefield, fighting for a common cause. It wasn't for the politicians, like so many hippies go on about . . . soldiers aren't politicians. They don't want to be. Maybe that's why soldiers fight."

Slim swirled his whiskey in the bottom of his glass. "Desensitize would be the closest word for it, you know? I mean, how else do you prepare a man for war? Most of the officers at Stoke Ridge wanted to be like Rambo—Dykes always bragged, but he'd never seen an actual war. But still, he yelled louder to hide it and then his voice would crack. Not just him, but all the officers: they couldn't communicate what it actually meant to kill. The closest they got was video games. As for the officers that had been to war, well, they were even worse off, only able to connect by reliving the things that had destroyed their humanity in the first place, you know? You've seen those commercials like it's Call of Duty? Can't do it like the old days. Too taxing. Too damaging. But you put a guy up in a helicopter and throw him some night-vision goggles and he'll shoot the grainy silhouettes on the ground, no problem. You ever wonder why I refuse to play all those shooters, Hugh? You don't want to know just how realistic they are."

It was The Beast's turn to hit the bathroom. All of us were mildly drunk. Slim told me how he got high during his first tour to cope: mostly weed, LSD, and mushrooms. He wasn't one for cocaine or ecstasy or pills, which he called soul-numbing drugs. When he got to UNC he dabbled in Adderall.

"But after I got hit in the jugular and came back, I wasn't particularly proud of fighting. See, *terrorist* is just a word they use to convince you to pull the trigger. I mean, how else are they supposed to get teenagers to shoot at twelve-year-old boys? It was a shitty situation, I know it. But I did what had to be done. Not in some philosophical sense, though I just had to survive. It's quite the scene in retrospect—I'm talking about when I got hit in the jugular and a bullet festered in my chest, Hugh."

With a couple dozen insurgents coming straight at him with AK-47s, Slim said he entered a state of Flow. When it became clear Slim was not only going to make it out of there but that his actions would be called heroic for a time, after he'd thrown back a makeshift grenade that exploded in midair, showering a group of fifteen-year-old attackers with a thousand spiked nails only to jump for cover behind a fallen soldier and use the corpse as cover, lifting the body and using it to charge a young insurgent who literally shit his pants before Slim gutted him with a bowie knife, after Slim had picked up a rock and thrown it square between the eyes of a well-respected Republican Guard commander and then proceeded to dive behind cover to radio-in a chopper and "GET ME THE FUCK OUTTA HERE!" before exhausting his M60 heavy machine gun to fill another fifteen or so insurgents with holes, now clutching his jugular wound with his left hand and firing his pistol with his right, not to even mention the unseemly amounts of blood exiting his heaving chest, well, the boy nicknamed Slim experienced a kind of transformation at the First Battle of Fallujah that provided a ticket out of Iraq and left him forever changed.

"Jesus," The Beast said. "And you went back?"

"You better believe it. But something spiritual had happened. Ain't no other way to describe it. It was like everything that had happened didn't matter anymore. I no longer thought about Dykes and my mom and all those years down at the creek. It was cleansing, in a way. So of course I wanted to get back. I heard the term once: autotelic experience. And there's nothing like facing death to make you feel alive. It became a drug, the Flow."

Slim was quiet for a few minutes before continuing. "Dykes tried to get at me in the hospital multiple times. Used different disguises even, but General Haith protected me. Always stayed by my bedside."

"General Haith? Why?"

"Haith was a good man. And I think he felt guilty about my injury, since he was the one who sent me to war. He told me not to worry though, that I was gonna be all right. He'd been in Vietnam and said you aren't free from what life throws at you, only in how you respond. That stuck with me, you know? So that's what I did—figured I'd go back to Iraq. Me and him visited my mom together before I shipped out."

"What'd she have to say for herself?"

"Nothing. She was dead." Slim wasn't affected by the phrase. "Who eats a batch of weed brownies before mowing the lawn? We found her, Haith and I. Dead in the grass, on the lawn. Seems she was high enough to walk in front of the mower—she never bought a blade protector and always kept the autopilot on. Her foot looked like diced onions when we found her. It had been at least a week. She stunk. She probably was too stoned to even feel it, watching the grass turn purple until she lost too much blood. I didn't feel much, to be honest . . . what I remember most was that the yard was overgrown and felt alive. General Haith called the coroner, and I packed up my things. I haven't been back since. When I shipped out, Haith said if I ever needed anything, I knew who to call. I haven't heard from him in years actually . . . I should get back in touch."

"You know what's most amazing though?" Slim continued. "They found a joint dangling from her mouth. Even while she was bleeding out like a stuck pig. I sold the trailer and all that was inside—everything except for some Playmobil and Lincoln Logs. And, well, you know the rest: I went back to Iraq to finish what I'd started. Distinguished Service Cross during Operation Together Forward. But they took away my medal anyway. I wasn't about to pull the trigger on two buses full of kids."

Slim shook his head. "How can you be proud of that? Serve your country and end up feeling like an asshole? Doesn't matter though, does it? Those boys and girls are still dead. Lot more dead kids too, now. Shit. And they keep calling 'em terrorists 'cause they're trying to defend their homeland. Anyway, when I enrolled at UNC, I tried to get past it. Getting lost in the books helped me forget. But the past has a way of creeping up on you, doesn't it? It's those memories that haunt you. Harder to forget at night. And it's easier to teach a man how to kill than to love. My mom never hugged me so I'm sure that caused a few problems . . . and Dykes's beatings didn't help either, so I have to thank Hugh for that." The Beast smiled. "Wasn't getting any support before The Skillet, what with Fox News saying I was a traitor for speaking out against Iraq and NPR telling me I was a traitor 'cause I killed civilians. But I didn't kill 'em, I tried to save 'em. At least I wanted to. So where in the hell you think all that frustration went when I got back? I didn't do coke but once. It gave me the runs. Just stuck to weed. And then I started hating myself for it, with my mom's death and all. You know how it is with intoxication—harder than you think to stop yourself. And that's something I realized after my first tour in Iraq—General Haith always said the hardest thing in life isn't recognizing your problems, it's that knowing where they come from doesn't make them easier to fight. Sometimes finding out the source makes it even *harder* to fix. So I can recognize where it comes from—my relationship with Dykes and all. But that doesn't necessarily help me move on."

The bar was muggy. We stepped outside. The breeze swayed and the wind chimes chimed. The dirt parking lot became spotted with infrequent raindrops. Like a swarm of locusts, gray sheets of rain appeared on the horizon.

9

A waft of must followed him in. Mothballs and booze: the consummate alcoholic. Despite his six-foot-five frame, or maybe because of it, Dykes had all the markings of a sad and pathetic man.

He hunched his shoulders when he walked and swung his arms like a gorilla and finished sentences with a question mark. His voice was nasally grating and tenuous. His gaze was that of an entitled pup—I don't mind saying it looked a lot like this: ☹. Come rain or come shine, the mosquitoes or the heat, you could be sure Dykes looked for a reason to complain. Dykes didn't care about rambling or getting too personal and spoke like he was making up for lost time. He had no chutzpah, no balls, no tact, and no charm. He woke up every day believing life had done him wrong, sighing when he arose and when he turned in for the night. And though he'd inherited a fortune and a mansion to boot, like his parents he never realized a bigger house means an emptier one, too. Without any ambition, purpose, or self-respect, Dykes found solace at Lockart's Bar, where he lubricated his sorrow with whiskey.

"But," I told Slim and The Beast, "there might be more to Dykes than meets the eye."

"No, there's less." Slim finished his drink.

"Well you can be sure I know him better than most . . ."

"What's your point?" Slim asked. "I already knew all of that."

"You don't know about his parents. And that means you don't know the half of it. Or the quarter of it, at least. You ever heard of the Painted Lake?"

"Can't say that I have. He never talked about his youth. He only ever mentioned Mr. Charles . . ."

"Ah, Mr. Charles," I said. "His chauffeur until thirteen. Apparently he liked to play marbles and watch Dykes dance . . ."

"You mentioned something about a lake?" The Beast asked.

"It used to be called Dykes Pond," I answered. "Renamed the Painted Lake on account of the LGBT community. It's quite the story. One second, I'll put some music on. Always nice to have a soundtrack, isn't it?"

For a moment no one spoke except for Robert Johnson—*You better come on, in my kitchen, well it's goin' to be rainin' outdoors.* Then I began to recount Dykes's story as Slim and The Beast listened along.

Sasha Dykes was a self-described *après-gardiste.* The term didn't exist outside of her mind. Less than one hundred people ever saw her art, but part of the allure was thinking her art was valuable 'cause it was rare. She'd been born Sasha Jenkins and had lived above the sewers of New York, just early enough to witness the twilight of the Dadaist movement. By eighteen she was calling herself a concept artist, taking pride in imaginary paintings and drawings that could hypothetically be drawn. Unaware that she had to believe in what she was doing, and while most Dadaist artists were moving on to surrealism, Sasha continued to take pride in her concepts. She was a buffoon, plain and simple, but she was also beautiful, which kept her on the fringes of the popular artist crowd. She wanted to seem nonchalant while doing everything to be seen; and so at twenty-three, when she met a rich man who liked expensive art by the name of Trent Dykes, she quickly fell in love in hopes of attending trendy galas where she could peddle her concepts to people who thought being artistic meant opining about art. Trent promised his newlywed she could do anything she wanted, and so they moved down to North Carolina next to a man-made pond.

What started as an empty relationship turned into an empty marriage. Trent wooed his bodacious lover with jewelry and fine wines. They slept back to back. They argued more than they hugged. Trent spent most of his time at work, where Sasha wouldn't be a bother; as Chandler could attest, he cheated on her all the time. Chandler walked in on his father receiving a blow job more than once—a maid in the laundry room, a catering staffer behind the woodshed (twice), and Sasha Dykes herself in Trent's air-conditioned office. "My mom always visited once a month," Dykes had told me on a particularly drunken night. "She usually didn't take me with her, but on this one day I came along. I was six. She told me to wait out in the hall. But there were noises, so I walked in and saw my mom on her knees under the desk, her ass sticking out from under it. She was wearing a skirt. I saw her panties and her thing bulging out . . . her head was bobbing up and down. I can still hear the slurping. I thought something was wrong. 'Mommy, what are you doing?' Trent looked up. He wasn't angry like the other times, though. He just sniggered and watched."

Dykes's voice cracked. "Are you a family man, Lockart?"

"You already asked me—"

"And you're a good husband, right? You wouldn't put your wife on a list. You wouldn't degrade mommy, right? That day he told me to stand there and watch. He whispered, 'Stand right there, Chandler. Stand right there and watch.' I don't know if mommy heard it, but she continued on. She was under the desk for ten minutes. She gagged while Trent pushed her head down. As she was choking Trent told me to get out. Five minutes later mommy left the room. I don't think she knew I'd been inside. It was 'our little secret,' Trent told me. One day I'd be proud. The car ride home was quiet. Mommy had a new necklace on."

Of course, Trent quickly grew tired of Sasha's mouth and built her a toy for her concept art: a large tower hanging over Dykes Pond. The thirty-foot wooden structure, like a medieval siege unit, had a rickety wooden ladder leading to a diving platform up top. It loomed over floating plastic cordons containing different colored paints—reds, blues, greens, and yellows like chocolate pudding skins atop the water. A camera on a tripod stood on the other side of the pond, set to time-capture the fateful day when Sasha would finally jump. She worked exclusively in a red and blue polka-dotted dress and spent most of her days in contemplation, dangling her feet off the edge of the tower. For years she just sat there, day in and day out. And then one day she decided to jump. Little Chandler witnessed it from his bedroom. Trent wasn't around. The splash was colorful, if underwhelming. Sasha quickly got out of the water and sprinted up the hill with her camera and put the singular photo into a scrapbook entitled "ART." After that fateful day, Sasha referred to herself as an artist, content with the moniker as her husband sat at a desk in a frigid office. He was a defense lawyer for a business that had something to do with testing drugs. He always kept the AC on lest he sweat profusely.

Trent Dykes enjoyed the fast-food strips and shopping malls, watching his bank account grow as his family grew apart. Sasha was oblivious and spent all of her time by the pond, ignorant of the needs of her child. She never breast-fed 'cause she was obsessed with her tits; when they started to sag she became depressed. Both Sasha and Trent drank heavily each night, usually red wine from a box. During the holidays, Trent stayed in luxury hotels "on business." His son learned about loneliness but not how to be alone. When I asked Chandler Dykes why he liked spending his evenings in the bathtub, he said it was 'cause of the warmth and the silence. Somehow he felt vindicated that his parents wouldn't know if he'd drowned, as if they'd finally care about him if he died. By seven years old he was making his own lunches. He never could trade for Dunkaroos in class. And then his parents hired a chauffeur named Mr. Charles who was always waiting for him at school at three o'clock on the dot. Charles made Chandler after-school snacks and often asked to play marbles. He played big band jazz music in the car. Sometimes, in the parking lot, Chandler danced for Mr. Charles. Other times the chauffeur taught Chandler to swing and do the Lindy Hop. During his tenth year Chandler developed quite a talent for drawing, but Sasha resented the fact that *her* drawings weren't as good as her son's, so she told him to find a different hobby and ripped his drawings off the fridge.

Every night was the same in the Dykes household: the wine came out from seven o'clock onwards, followed by yelling and then grunting before it became quiet. Sasha and Trent always debated who should be taking care of "the child." Sasha argued that her art was what kept her alive and that it would be blasphemous to stop working at the pond, whereas Trent said his money was what fueled her "so-called art" and that *he* was the one who paid the Y to look after "the child." Chandler listened from a fetal position in the bathtub, later running the bath water to drown out his father's late-night grunts. As the child slowly grew up, Trent spent more and more nights "away on business," while Sasha seemed happy contemplating by the pond. They rarely saw the child during those years, not least 'cause they never drove him to or from school. Chandler grew to hate Mr. Charles 'cause he always turned around to look at Chandler at red lights, asking him if he'd like to stop off somewhere to dance or play marbles.

And then, on a particularly rainy day when Chandler was twelve, he fell asleep in the bathtub and almost drowned.

"So he tried to kill himself?" The Beast asked.

"That's not how he saw it," I replied. "He never told me if he'd done it on purpose, just that he 'wanted to fall asleep, turn it off.' Sasha pulled him out of the bathtub and slapped him into consciousness. The only reason she came in was 'cause she needed help at the pond. Leading her son by the wrist down to the water, Sasha told Chandler to get the containment booms out of the water. That was the final straw, Dykes said. He stopped coming home at all. He stole a key from a janitor and started sleeping at the Y in the director's office. Soon enough his father sent him to Stoke Ridge."

Robert Johnson crooned: *Wonder could I bear apologize? Or would she sympathize with me? Wonder could I bear apologize* . . . I glanced outside. It was summer all right, but dusk was coming on. It was as if someone had dimmed the lights.

Slim and The Beast walked to the window.

"We won't make it to Asheville before it hits," The Beast said.

The sky looked mean. Black clouds rolled in and grumbled about. The wind lashed the windows. The rain had started up. While the lightning remained hidden, thunder began to vibrate along the rooftop.

Being drunk leads to curiosity more than concern.

"You think it's worse than Fran?" Slim asked. "I haven't seen a real storm in years . . ."

"Neither have I," The Beast said. "I say we wait it out."

"If need be, you boys are welcome to stay here," I offered. "At least until the eye of the storm. There's a bedroom upstairs. My wife will be coming around to give us the update, anyhow."

Robert Johnson plucked his strings for a time.

"So what happened then?" The Beast sipped a fresh whiskey. "Is Sasha still out by the pond?"

"Well no, not really," I said. "Sasha decided to jump."

After years of contemplating a second splash, I continued, Sasha Dykes decided to make her art public. Chandler was fourteen, home for vacation from Stoke Ridge. I think it was actually Trent who coerced Sasha into taking the plunge; see, partygoers were no longer impressed with Sasha's concept art, and Trent had his own reasons for collecting the event funds. He promised her more jewelry and Botox, but in the end she didn't have a choice, or so it seemed. He planned the party weeks before even asking for her thoughts, and North Carolina's rich and beautiful poured thousands into the *The Painted Lake: The Gravity is Art Project* to finally *see* Sasha's art. It's possible Sasha knew it wasn't wise, but she probably wanted the recognition. The main event was to be centered on a seventy-six-foot fall, guaranteeing the most impressive of splashes. Even though there was a twenty- and forty-five-foot option, Sasha was quite specific about the height. And as she climbed the ladder to reach the summit, looking down at the newly bought rubber containment booms filled with reds, greens, blues, and yellows, Sasha waved at her husband and all of her followers. Double-chinned men and bejeweled Barbies looked on, drinking spritzy mimosas in the NC sun. At the top of the structure, Sasha removed the faded polka-dot dress and let it float down to the water. Her body was pale. She was unhealthily gaunt. A collection of brittle bones in loose skin. And maybe she was happy to climb to the top; or maybe she was scared to finally share her art; or maybe being watched by so many people tricked her into ignoring what was truly important there. Whatever the reason, she jumped and screamed triumphant. Her shriek sent a chill down her son's pubescent spine. And perhaps a balding CEO pricked his gums with a toothpick; and maybe a waiter asked, "How deep is that pond?" To be sure, her husband chuckled as Sasha careened toward the water. The splash was majestic. Paint spewed up from the pond. A volcanic eruption of Sasha's art. Having never jumped from such heights themselves, no one questioned the bedrock. They would've clapped if not for the glasses in their hands, waiting in silence for a fist to emerge from the water.

But Sasha never came up. Cracked skull, plain and simple. Chandler gasped from his bedroom as spectators looked on. It took a couple minutes for Trent Dykes to jump into the water; by the time he came sputtering up, everyone knew something was wrong. The men held their breath. Most of the women gasped. It's a myth that dead bodies float in the water. The guests stared blankly at each other and the pond. Two members of the wait staff dove to the bottom. Once they'd dragged Sasha's limp body onto the shore, they covered her bloodied head with a towel. For many of the guests this was the first Bad Thing they'd ever seen; and so after hours of speaking to local news crews, recounting what had happened as if they'd been personally affected by the tragedy—as if they needed therapy to try and make sense of it all—all of the men returned to their offices and the art-buying folk back to Williamsburg and Manhattan, where they sat in their loft apartments filled with floor pillows and Smartwater bottles to talk about how amazing it was to see someone literally die for her art and how *that* was true art and how the pop stars of today could learn a thing or two from the heroic Sasha Dykes, the woman who'd sacrificed her life to *say something important* and was, in the words of a mustachioed concept artist, "a hero amongst us all." The pond was soon drained and filled in with earth. Trent was left alone to rot in his mansion (from that day onward Chandler stayed at Stoke Ridge during holidays), but soon ran out of money and moved to New York, where he continued to work in medical malpractice for a time before dying in one of those Chinatown bus accidents.

"She didn't put her husband in the will?" The Beast asked.

"Not a penny," I replied. "Everything went to Chandler. But he was still a minor, couldn't touch the trust fund until eighteen. Trent moved to New York with what little he had left and waited for his son's eighteenth birthday to try and cash in."

The Beast shook his head. "You've gotta feel for the guy though, right? He didn't say anything about his mom?"

"Nothing at first. Said he had no need for mourning back then . . ."

I've got stones in my passway, my road seems dark as night . . . filled the silence in the bar.

10

Jennifer Dawton and Winston Fields used to run a quaint diner off Old Highway 86. It was a long, winding road slicing through dense forests and meadows grazed by cows and other four-legged creatures. The barns used to hold horses and pigs and cows, but by the time The Beast was born, there were only machines. Still, when the Dawton-Fields relocated back in the eighties, there were no sub-divisions or shopping centers or cookie-cutter homes. Just tick-infested forests filled with agile and frightened deer, verdant meadows and golden pastures covered in rolls of hay, and everywhere the cicadas chirping and the bees buzzing amid the quiet rustle of trees and pollen irritating the eyes and thunderstorms flooding shallow waters. The region used to be filled with people who knew the lay of the land: they didn't wear earplugs to use a lawn mower or goggles to use a tractor or gloves to tend to livestock or bug spray in the yard. The Dawton-Fields bought local, but not 'cause they were acting: "going green" was as obvious as dishwashing by hand.

Their beloved restaurant was called Chez Moi. It stood alone in a clearing, down a dusty road lined with grass. It was a small two-story home with a screened in porch. The first floor had been renovated to have the feel of a classic diner; the tables were small and round like in French cafés, and the waiters didn't bring the check unless asked twice. "The goal was a memorable experience," The Beast recalled. "And part of that experience is losing track of time." Chez Moi was a favorite among local artists, who often sat on the porch in white rocking chairs and drank sweet tea. It was a popular place on account of the family feel and the honest prices, but those who knew about cuisine also knew about this French secret down south. According to *Southern Living*, Chez Moi was among the best in French fusion cuisine on account of its "haute-cuisine creations with a down home feel." The Dawton-Fields won multiple awards for the place, including *Southern Living*'s Meal of the Year Award for their honey-glazed duck breast in a red wine reduction alongside a goat cheese soufflé and the chef's choice of wine.

Jennifer Dawton had started out as a bio major before falling in love with cooking. Once she graduated from Duke University in the midsixties, she moved with her fiancée Winston to Paris. And there, under the trees of Canal Saint Martin and in the Luxembourg Gardens, they drank Côtes du Rhône and frequented the famous Marché de Rungis, learning how to properly sear a duck, grill shrimp, and roast a chicken, how to pick the right sauces for a steak tartare and how to judge a baguette by bringing it right up to the ear and giving it a slight squeeze in the middle to verify the crunch. They became master chefs in Paris and then moved back to North Carolina to start a family. When Hugh Dawton-Fields was born, he didn't scream. The nurse said he had some kind of mischief in his eyes, and as a boy he snuck away to be alone after dinner.

"They moved to downtown Carrboro in the beginning," The Beast recalled. "Lived with a couple of hippies. But they didn't like having to always eat vegan, not for long, so they bought a place in the countryside and started Chez Moi."

Jennifer and Winston renovated the whole place. Winston literally broke his back once when he fell from a ladder. Chez Moi was finished by the time Hugh turned three, and within six months they were able to buy a second place down the street, keeping the upstairs bedroom to sleep in on busy weekend nights. "They built a small bedroom right above the kitchen." The Beast paused for a moment. He swallowed hard. "We slept there when the restaurant was especially busy. I slept on two sleeping bags, bordered by pillows on the floor." Slim listened intently. He hadn't heard this before.

After a year of smooth sailing, Hugh had a bad eczema outbreak that demanded his parents' full attention. "Once I got better they reopened the restaurant and started to work weekends again. But they never went back to full-time . . . they knew how important it was for me to have them around. I was shy when I started school and got made fun of for being so tall. The only thing I had then was the basketball court."

"How tall were you?" Slim asked.

"Five feet five by the time I was ten."

"Was that where you got the nickname?" I asked.

"The Beast? No. They called me Mr. Munster."

"From the show on *Nick at Nite*?" Slim wondered.

"Yeah. 'Cause of my deep voice, too. I didn't really hang around other kids until I was fifteen. I didn't mind it though . . . mostly remember helping out in the kitchen and playing basketball out back. I liked being alone."

"You spent all day playing?"

"All day basketball. All night cooking."

"And your parents didn't worry about you being lonely?" Slim asked.

"No, I was happy. I preferred spending time on my own. They figured I'd grow into myself."

"And what about the kids at school?"

"Well yeah, my parents worried. No one wants to see their kid getting called names. But what were they gonna do? They couldn't sit there with me in class and defend me. They just made sure to ask me how my day was when I got home. Not just what I did, but how I actually felt. They were more like friends, really. They instilled the lessons early on."

If they'd had a bad day, they'd honor it instead of suppress it—instead of taking out their frustration on him when he spilled the milk, they'd sit the four-year-old down and explain how if-we-seem-upset-honey-well-it's-not-your-fault-it's-just-been-a-tough-day-at-the-restaurant-'cause-the-steamer's-broken. And even though the four-year-old could barely understand what they were saying, he could *feel* that their frustration wasn't about him; and if there were a problem between Jennifer and Winston—say, a screaming match over when it was best to clean the kitchen—they'd apologize for the cursing and the yelling and conclude that in the end the best strategy is to clean as you cook. Since The Beast's parents treated their child with respect and responsibility, they never made him pick sides and it was never about who could win. Cooking was the primary teaching tool for their child, but not the last. The rule in the kitchen was simple enough: if someone was cooking, *everyone* was cooking. So from six-years-old onward, Hugh made the salad dressing while Jennifer cut the vegetables and his father layered the lasagna.

"They always told me it was paramount to stay focused on the task. To take care with everything, from preparation to presentation to cleaning up *before* the meal was ready. Multitasking was fine as long as I made sure never to leave the handle of the frying pan sticking out, 'cause one of their friends did that once and burned the kitchen down."

The Dawton-Fields brought out the best in each other. Winston helped Jennifer keep the kitchen clean, while Jennifer made sure the table was set, lest the food be ready but not the meal. Jennifer poured wine into small decanters and often garnished the dishes with bay or mint leaves; each time they sat down for dinner, they held each other's hands in a circle, sharing a moment of silence before digging in. The Dawton-Fields made a choice to live actively instead of passively, a belief that wasn't hard to engender in a child who liked to learn. They taught their child to go through life with purpose, setting a limit to playing video games and explaining the importance of making the bed. The best way to make a change is to shift the perspective, they showed him; and so The Beast learned about tolerance and tolerating intolerance at school, and though he didn't agree, he understood it just the same.

"What'd you just say?" Slim interrupted. "Tolerating intolerance? What does that mean? You aren't exactly an angel on the basketball court, Hugh . . ."

"Yeah, of course. I don't deny it. But a kid isn't just the product of his parents, right? You forget: I went to public schools. And I wasn't a popular kid. So even if I liked being quiet and alone, I have a side that flares out, too."

Perhaps the primary danger of pursuing their passion was sacrificing certain luxuries for their child. The Beast attended an overcrowded and underfunded public school where disillusioned and underpaid teachers knew him by his last name . . . "So big surprise that I was lost when I got to high school. I was just going through puberty. I was unsure of who I was becoming. My whole body was changing and I had no idea what was going on. How do you tell a kid to be comfortable when he's seven feet tall? I grew nine inches in less than two years, so that's when I started getting a lot of attention for basketball. I was six feet eight by then. The varsity coach wanted me on the team. He'd never seen me play but figured he could use me . . . and there was a girl I liked. As the cliché goes she was a cheerleader, so I said I'd give it a shot, and overnight the whole school respected me. Not for the right reasons, but it still felt good . . . but I never really adjusted, I don't think."

"You mean to the organized game, or socially?"

"Oh, organized game I dominated. Except for the fouls."

"So what about the girl?"

"It was a disaster pretty much immediately. I mean, I got her, if by that you mean I kissed her. But I didn't know what I was doing. I just kept my mouth open. It was like a vacuum. Inside the echo of her breathing. She moved her tongue around. It was weird. So that was it for me. She told everyone about it. I didn't have sex until I was eighteen . . ."

"Yeah, I didn't make out with anyone 'til I was sixteen, either," Slim said. "But once that happened, everything came quickly."

"I was shy," The Beast replied. "I wasn't exactly popular. I mean, on the basketball court I was, but I didn't do anything on weekends. Helped my parents at the restaurant for a part-time job. Kept me distracted, plus I loved cooking."

"And your teammates?" I asked. "They weren't your friends either?"

"Not really, no. They'd known each other since they were six. Always hung out after games, but never invited me. Plus they were way too serious about it, basketball that is . . . they were into AAU and all the Nike camps and stuff. So I didn't have the team spirit coach always talked about . . . still played like I was in the backyard. For fun, that's it. But I was seven feet, so the talent was secondary. I didn't have to try to be the best in the state—my size took care of that. I'd watched Jordan highlights since I was a kid, too. In the beginning I was too aggressive, partly 'cause I wanted to get back at the same kids that had made fun of me and called me Mr. Munster. But I got over that pretty quickly, mostly because they were on my team. And I was so much bigger than all of them . . . in practice I had to make sure not to injure them."

"So that's where you got the nickname?"

"Yeah. Somewhere along the way. I broke a teammate's nose by accident. Or maybe it was his wrist."

"By accident?" Slim asked.

"Yeah, well . . . I wanted to hurt him, but not that badly."

"What'd he do?"

"He made fun of my hyphenated name."

"So you never made close friends?"

"Not really. It was all surface level. Most of them were just using me—they knew I'd end up playing in college. Senior year I was popular, but only because I wanted to be. When you're tall and you play sports, you're one of the cool kids automatically. It didn't last long, but I still had my stint. The only thing I was never allowed to do was talk to the media."

And the scouts sure did come. They called the Dawton-Fieldses' residence day and night in hopes of acquiring the biggest name in the high school game. "It was crazy the amount of attention I got once people started thinking about money. Even before I had a single pubic hair they were saying I was the next great big man in the game. They were saying I was the best center to come out of high school since Shaq. And that was with Dwight Howard drafted the previous year. But in 2006, that changed . . . couldn't draft straight out of high school anymore. My parents were secretly thankful for that—at least it quelled some of the noise."

"Why wouldn't they let you talk to anyone?"

"They didn't think it was in my best interest. They didn't trust anyone who was willing to bribe a teenager. And they got sick of it really quickly, what with the phone ringing day and night. They never let me do magazine covers or any of that. Even interviews. They said I was too young, that it wasn't good to have so much attention. And I was fine with that. I didn't want to have 'an image' anyway."

"But it was going to be your career . . ."

"They were excited for me, sure. But they also had a restaurant to manage. And I was going to get a degree. That wasn't even a discussion. I always knew I'd finish at UNC. As for all the hype, I got over that in high school."

"What about the girls?" Slim asked. "How the hell did you not have sex until eighteen?"

"Because I was awkward and they were fake. I didn't know how to pretend to make a connection. So I stuck to myself after games, and I didn't go out and celebrate. And everyone thought it was because I was so driven, so motivated to improve my game . . . but, to be honest, it was because I preferred being quiet. It's exhausting to have people staring at you all the time. That's why I feel so bad for beautiful women. I preferred spending weekends in the kitchen. You know, I didn't live and breathe the game like others did. I love the game, sure. But I know I also want to do other things. Paradoxically, since it was *just a game* to me, I never got nervous. I didn't fold under pressure. Ten minutes or ten seconds . . . it didn't matter. The competition was easy, and so the main reason for being benched at the end of games was I didn't need to be in. Everyone knew about me without knowing who I was, you know? Since I never talked to the media all they could do was make predictions. Scouts were always at Chez Moi, or sitting outside of my house in black Escalades. There was this one recruiter who was incessant. University of Tennessee. He spent two years at the restaurant, coming every weekend. Fakest smile I've ever seen. My mom finally put a laxative in his shrimp and grits."

"So how'd you end up at UNC?" I asked.

"It was the only school that didn't pressure me. Duke was nice too, but they already had a stacked front court and I wanted to play immediately. Plus, UNC was closer to my parent's restaurant, so I could help out on weekends. But honestly, it was because I had a better guided tour at UNC than Duke. In Durham the tour guide had too many teeth in his mouth. And it rained. Those are the main reasons, really. There's no grandiose history."

"I remember being a freshman and seeing those T-shirts: 'Dawn of The Beast'," Slim recalled.

"Yeah, that's when the nickname really caught on. The high school state championship was broadcast on national TV. I dominated the game—thirty and twenty, something like that—but I also broke a kid's nose by accident. Elbowed him in the face. He was on my team. Went up for a rebound and accidentally hit him. From then on I was known by my nickname. T-shirts and posters and all the rest of it. But even then, it didn't get to me. It was kind of surreal at UNC: Dick Vitale screaming, "IT'S THE BEAST, BABY!"; watching my teammates praying, covering their eyes at the ends of close games. You know that feeling when you're at a really good party and still all you want to do is leave? Like the more you drink, the more sober you feel?"

"Did your parents ever watch?" I asked.

"Every single game."

"And what did they think?"

"They loved watching me, but for them it was also just a game. They knew me better than anyone else in the world and sensed I didn't feel it. Not that I didn't like it, just that my life didn't end with the result of the game. Now, that doesn't mean my dad didn't bite his fingernails and occasionally scream. But neither of them ever really seemed interested in the competition. One of the last things my dad ever said to me was a quote by Dr. J: 'Being a professional is doing the things you love to do on the days you don't feel like doing them.'"

Slim couldn't help but amend the phrase. "Yeah, that and a couple growth spurts, a forty-inch vertical, and a massive wing span. Not to mention staying healthy . . ."

"I still think about that sentence every day."

Despite the jovial music in the background—I'd switched to Django Reinhardt—the energy had shifted. I made a point to turn the music down to where it wouldn't overpower the speech. The rain's patter on the roof and the thunder outside were more appropriate for The Beast's tone.

"The night they died we got in a fight. I was there, working late. They were teaching me a new recipe."

Slim held his breath. He'd never heard this confession before.

"I don't know what started the fire." The Beast kept his eyes on the bar. "Maybe a gas leak. It was an accident, that's all. I just wish we hadn't gotten in a fight that night. I was so stupid . . . I was frustrated because I couldn't get the recipe right. They told me I wasn't ready to cook for the restaurant, but I wanted to prove them wrong. And that's when my dad quoted Dr. J again—he said I couldn't just walk in here and expect it to work out. He said cooking takes patience and experience and time. And my poor mom was just trying to help out . . . she said not to think of it as a competition . . . that I had to cook with love. And I knew it was true, but it sounded so patronizing.

She was always so optimistic. So I yelled at her. That's when my dad told me to get out of the kitchen, and so I shoved him. He fell back into a shelf and knocked over a couple of pots. I said I was sick of cooking for them. That I was done with the restaurant. I can still see my mom's eyes—that's what kills me. Even then, at that moment, she managed to smile. She was calm. 'Get some sleep, Hugh,' she said. She put her hand on my shoulder, and was gone. And then I got even angrier because I knew I'd fucked up. That was the last night I ever saw them."

The Beast's voice was shaky. You could hear the tears being held back. "And then my dad just sat there and listened to me yell. He never said anything. Not once. After I finished ranting about who knows what, he went upstairs without saying anything, and then he was also gone."

A few minutes passed before The Beast continued. The Beast's eyes remained glued to the bar. "The worst thing is, I didn't even know why I did it. Sometimes I get frustrated and can't control it, that's all. There was a time when I couldn't do much of anything but sit and stare at the wall. I ate meatloaf with mashed potatoes and green peas for weeks. I made huge batches of it, so I wouldn't have to cook much. Coach Brees came a few times to leave groceries, but he kept insisting we talk about it, trying to force me to move on. After a few weeks, though, I figured I had to get out of the house. So I went to the grocery store and decided to go through all of the family recipes."

He seared duck and grilled summer vegetables; he sautéed prawns and stuffed tomatoes; he fried gnocchi with onions and zucchinis marinated in Moroccan spices and crème fraîche; he made tortellini stuffed with lobster and sun-dried tomatoes; he drizzled the finest olive oil, balsamic vinegar, and mustard concoction on top of summer salads made with apples seared with honey and onions; he took care not

only to make the food, but also to present it as his own, often apply-
ing his father's technique of flipping a small white bowl filled with
rice upside down, placing golden-brown onions placed ever-so-gently
on top of a homemade burger topped with a dash of sea salt and
perhaps a blade of grass for decoration, or hanging a single bay leaf
on an oven-baked chicken breast, not 'cause he ate it, but 'cause the
aesthetic was also important, and "only then, once it's decorated, can
you slice through the meat with the edge of your fork."

For weeks The Beast cooked in solitude, reading the family cookbooks. He became an amateur chef in the Latin sense of the word,
loving every minute, shedding more than a few tears along the way.
He sat alone in his living room, where they once celebrated Christmas.
He listened to Chet Baker or Miles Davis and took his time eating,
as if every bite or sip kept the memory of his parents alive. For six
months, The Beast sat in his father's chair and rested his feet on his
mother's yellow balance ball, reminiscing about how he used to jump
in his parents' bed and play gymnastics in the morning, how his father
used to lift him towards the basketball hoop or lie flat on his back
and hold him above his head, and how Jennifer used to gently press
on his eyelids just before he fell asleep. The Beast cleaned the kitchen
with as much care as he took to prepare: he never used the dishwasher
and dried each pot and pan by hand; then he'd brew himself a cup
of Earl Grey tea, just like his father used to make, taking care to put
the sugar and the tea bag in first, then pour in the water and five
minutes later add the milk. The Beast performed these rituals each
and every day, never talking or needing to explain.

"After a few months I returned to the Dean Dome. I wanted to
finish out my senior year and then declare for the draft."

Secretly, I hoped The Beast would mention the Jim Brees Incident.
It wasn't so much curiosity as a need for the story to be complete. But

neither Slim nor I asked what happened that day. Like Sgt. Dykes, we were left guessing why The Beast put his coach in a three-week coma.

11

"You know I went to Dykes's cabin just once," I told Slim and The Beast after putting on James Taylor's *Sweet Baby James*. "He'd left his Velcro wallet in my bar. He didn't come back the next day, or the day after, which was strange. When he didn't answer the front door, I decided to look around."

It was a cold night in December, I recounted. The ground was covered in frost. My breath was silver in the forest 'cause the moonlight was strong. I peered through a window into the living room: crumpled papers, strewn peanuts, empty pizza boxes, and Red Label Johnny Walker bottles covering the floor. There was an old Toshiba TV, too, illuminating the room with its fuzzy gray screen. I squinted at cut-out news stories, which covered the mahogany carpet: tales of Slim's military discharge, the war in Iraq, restaurant reviews of Chez Moi, local articles about The Beast's career at UNC and Jim Brees, and one entitled "What Went Wrong?" There was also a collection of cut-out headlines taped to the wall: "Hometown Hero Turns to Drugs"; "Jim Brees Pleads Silence"; "Stoke Ridge Military Academy to Hold Memorial for General Don B. Haith."

"Haith?" Slim asked.

"I'm afraid so, Slim. It seems he died in a fire just last fall."

"Fire? What do you mean?"

"The authorities said it was an arsonist. But you know how it goes . . . arsonists rarely get caught."

As soon as I said it, I had a sinking feeling in my gut. I'd heard the same phrase the previous year; Dykes had smelled like gasoline. Still, I didn't want to scare Slim and The Beast by suggesting the sergeant murdered General Haith. I kept quiet.

"Anyhow, his cabin is creepy, I'll tell you that much. There was little else in the living room save a yellow pillow and dirty laundry. In the bedroom, a mattress and a single red lamp on the floor. The lamp head craned, beaming toward images on the wall: pictures of you two boys threaded together with red string. The pictures of you, Slim, were mostly Polaroids. Most of them had your face cut out . . . like he took your face off the body and glued it back on."

"What the fuck?"

"Same for you, Hugh, except with those low-quality Internet print-outs. In all of the pictures your heads had been pasted back on. There were newspaper and Internet articles highlighted in red, too. But they hadn't been cut out. I couldn't read most of 'em, what with the lamp's glare, but there was one document in the center of the wall that was easy to make out. It was like the centerpiece, the cornerstone: a list filled with bold, black names:

BAM LIST
SLIM
MOM AND DAD
~~GENERAL HAITH~~
~~SADDAM~~
THE FACEBOOK TEAM
THE BEAST.

"What a fucking creep," Slim said, "he had that same list in his office at Stoke Ridge."

"And you said General Haith's name was crossed off?" The Beast asked.

"Him and Saddam," I replied. "As I was studying it, I heard this loud, hissing sound. Like a snake or something . . . I nearly fell down. I noticed some type of dog cage with a couple pizza boxes on top of it, so I peered in the next window to get a closer look. There was something inside, hissing, skulking around. I tapped on the window and that's when it lashed out—"

"Was it a cat?"

"I wish. A fiendish opossum. Started slamming itself up against the cage, sticking its snout through the grating, hissing and gnawing at the metal, trying every which way to get out. Razor sharp teeth as well . . . too many in its mouth."

"Jesus," The Beast said. "I didn't think you could domesticate an opossum?"

"Oh, it wasn't domesticated. Might as well have had rabies."

"Dykes had a stuffed one of those down at Stoke Ridge," Slim said, "he called him Larry."

"Well there you have it," I said, "he's always asking if he can bring

Larry some peanuts. A terrifying creature. Anyway, I still had Dykes's wallet in my back pocket, right? And after seeing the cut-out faces and Larry the opossum, I wasn't trying to stick around. But just as I was leaving, I peered through the kitchen and noticed a light: a thin, flickering beam creeping out from under the bathroom door. I walked around to the other side of the cabin and stood on my tippy-toes to see what was inside. I looked through the window, which was right above a running bathtub. I could only see by the flicker of a candle. Don't freak out now, all right? But there he was, naked, his back against the bathtub, suckling on an empty bottle of whiskey, staring at his laptop. His back was toward me, so he didn't see me. He was touching himself and rifling through porn pictures, mostly blow jobs. The faces didn't look right, though. Then I realized what was going on. You know how he cut out those pictures of you in the living room? Well now I know why. Your heads were photoshopped."

It took a moment for Slim and The Beast to grasp what I'd said. "When he came in the next day his eyes were dark and hollow," I said. "His fingers translucent and pruned. He was still somewhat wet. He dripped onto the bar even though it wasn't raining. When I leaned over to wipe the water off, he placed his right forearm next to mine: even that was wilted and translucent. Too skinny for a grown man's. 'Yours is so much bigger than mine,' he said. 'I have a condition, Lockart.' Then he tried to rub arms with me. He said he'd fallen asleep on it one night . . . woke up the next morning and couldn't feel a thing. Paralyzed for two months, he told me. Said he had to get the muscle back, somehow. I didn't respond, just kept quiet."

"'Pushups. You like 'em Lockart?' he asked me. 'I mean, do you do them?' He kneeled down on the floor. 'You know I can do over five hundred a day?' He lay down on his chest and looked up at the bar. He got real red faced and collapsed after nine or ten. Then he stood up again and shoved his withered arm back into my face. It was pale and smelled like fingernails. I told him to get his hand out of my face. He got offended and backed off. Was breathing really hard. He went back to his laptop in the corner under *Nighthawks*. Spent the next three hours surfing the Internet. He was bipolar like that—sometimes talkative, sometimes not. He'd sit for hours in silence, staring at the screen, squinting through the digital ether. He also often talked to himself under his breath. When the Wi-Fi connection was strong he'd watch videos and cheer on body builders—"

"Don't need to tell me twice," Slim recalled. "I can see it just fine. He usually stayed in his office and worked late into the night. Whenever he forced me to sleep there . . . I can still see the blue hue. He wore that white Titleist hat, color of piss-yellow. And a pair of runner's sunglasses just above the hat brim, placed on his forehead like a second pair of eyes. Does he still wear that '87 ACC Tournament Finals T-shirt? He must have a closet like Doug Funnie. Come to think of it, I don't think I ever saw him wear anything else. So did Dykes ever tell you where he went after getting kicked out of Stoke Ridge? 'Cause there were a couple of years before he moved out back behind the bar, weren't there? Or, was he just stalking me and Hugh the whole time?"

"After your award ceremony debacle he lived as a vagrant for a time," I responded. "Taking advantage of soup kitchens, homeless shelters, and the like. I don't think it was 'cause of money—he had that hefty inheritance—but he liked playing the victim nonetheless. He could've bought a place if he'd wanted to, I'm sure, but he seemed to prefer living like a vagabond and a drunk. Even now—he isn't exactly living beyond his means. He likes living on the outskirts—"

"Just like Stoke Ridge," Slim said.

"Not to mention being close to a bar, the free Wi-Fi, and that school down the road."

"Why a school?" The Beast asked.

"He likes to watch 'em work out," Slim replied.

"That, or just play," I explained. "He's admitted it before. Doesn't seem to find anything wrong with it. But as far as moving out here, it's probably just coincidence that there's a school. In the end he's a lonesome drunk who bought a place next to a bar. Like I said, when he first came in, I barely spoke to him. That lasted a few months. He was always on his laptop. He just paid for his drinks and sat online. He'd sit right over there, at the corner table, staring at the monitor like he was solving a complicated math problem, sipping Red Label, muttering to himself. I remember he liked to stick his tongue out the side of his mouth—"

"He did the same thing when he watched us work out," Slim said.

"He was polite enough, and quiet, but I never saw him smile. After all that time being online, he didn't seem to get any pleasure out of it. Always left the place frustrated and drunk. The more connections he made, the less connected he felt, I'd imagine. By the time he started talking to me, he bragged about having eight hundred Facebook friends. He'd post up at the bar and scroll through Facebook feeds to show me photos and status updates, occasionally writing on cadets' walls. At first I was polite. Soon enough I told him to stop showing me what he did online. More than anything else, though, he just watched, his eyes fixated on the screen, constantly reloading the page, waiting for someone to respond."

"Iatrogenesis," The Beast said offhandedly.

"Iatro what?"

"Iatrogenesis. That's what it sounds like. Opposite effect of what he wants. Lone-wolf leader of some digital pack. Iatrogenesis. Good word, look it up. Someone compared it to a Catch-22."

Slim laughed. "You'll have to excuse him, Lockart. Sometimes he starts talking nonsense like that. Using big words without explaining 'em . . . hard to know what he's saying—"

"It means sickness caused by medical treatment. Trying to combat the sickness becomes the cause. So Dykes—"

"What Hugh means to say is a paradox," Slim said. "It's like having a sweating problem 'cause you're nervous about having a sweating problem. DFW, right? Or not being able to have an orgasm 'cause you're thinking about not being able to have one."

The Beast conceded. "Yeah, I guess. Still, better to have one word that encompasses it all . . ."

"Not if nobody understands what you're talking about."

Slim and The Beast paused for a thunderclap. The rain on the roof was like silence.

Slim laughed. He was tipsy. "Man. Now *this* is a paradox: we left early to get out, and now we're smack dab in the middle of a hurricane and Dykes is next door. What an idiot, trying to find me on his laptop . . . Doesn't he know I don't have Facebook? It's not like Hugh would talk to him either . . ."

"Quinbee Nelson," I said.

"What?" The Beast responded.

"Quinbee Nelson. That's his alias. His digital self—has different names on email addresses and everything."

The Beast perked up. "That'd explain all the messages. Ever since last summer, a Quinbee Nelson's been pestering me. Literally hundreds of messages before I figured out how to block him. I just figured he was some crazy nut."

"For a time I cut off the Wi-Fi," I said. "But then he'd started jabbering on about Stoke Ridge and the letter that changed it all."

I explained that during his thirteenth year, Dykes began sleeping in the director's office at the Y. Secretly, of course; and it wasn't every night. "But it was frequent enough, it would seem. It might've been different if he hadn't been caught."

"That was the glory year," Chandler once said. He'd been working as an adolescent volunteer, coach, and spotter during the day, using the dirty towels to make a small nest for himself under the director's desk at night. At first no one caught on 'cause he was just an early riser enthusiastic about working out. The staff didn't mind either 'cause he always brewed them coffee. But when puberty took its course, the allure of nostalgia turned into an addiction. After kids started coming home with stories about shirtless workouts, Chandler received a lifetime ban from the Y for un-Christian behavior.

"That's when they realized he'd been sleeping in the office," I said. "And not just that; he'd also forced kids to sleep over and work out. One of them in particular. The rumor was he'd tried to touch him. Dykes denied it, of course, called it a misunderstanding." Slim shifted uncomfortably in his seat. "But before charges could be pressed, his dad sent him to Stoke Ridge Military Academy. They shaved his head and made fun of him . . . and without a bathtub for respite? Chandler whimpered himself to sleep in the communal shower each night. But this didn't go down well in the military academy: the other cadets threw soap bars at him and called him a faggot. They also beat and teased him. And after three boys cornered him in the showers and told him to get on his knees, he made a decision, there and then, to become the strongest cadet Stoke Ridge had ever seen. From that day forward all he did was work out. He instilled fear in the younger kids by challenging them to pushup contests. He beat them up when they failed and threw soap *at them* in the showers. He called them faggots and pussies for not running late-night. General Haith tried to discipline him, banning him from the weight room and from sports teams, but Dykes just did pushups and put Haith on the B.A.M. LIST. He'd found his niche. His peers began to fear him—"

"That was the only rule with Dykes's Tykes," Slim cut in. "Fear over all."

"Better to be feared than loved . . . isn't that Machiavelli?" The Beast wondered.

"Call it Machiavelli or call it the military. Fear and violence have always been the norm out in bum-fuck North Carolina. You wouldn't believe the number of times he specifically took us out to bars to start fights. Friday night was Fight Night, usually against drunken college kids. It was either that or fight Dykes himself. He always talked about World War Two and the no-retreat policy of the Russians."

Dykes still kept in contact with his father while at Stoke Ridge, more out of fear than anything else. He graduated friendless and applied to various colleges. His dream school was NC State—they had a fitness-design program there—but NC State wasn't on Trent's list of worthy colleges.

"The real tragedy was he got accepted," I imparted. "But I guess he was too afraid to defy his father."

"Why'd he stay at Stoke Ridge?" The Beast asked.

"The deal was, if he stayed Trent would get him a job. Trent had given a generous donation to Stoke Ridge, so he finagled to get Chandler a small office."

"But wait a minute," Slim added. "Dykes was eighteen by then. What happened to the trust fund? He could've done whatever he wanted."

"Right, the trust fund. Well Chandler loved Stoke Ridge," I replied.

"It was the only real family he'd known aside from the Y. Plus he didn't truly know how much Sasha had left him—probably believed it was the equivalent of monthly allowance. See, Trent convinced Chandler to give him access to the fund, said he would use it to invest . . . Trent also bought his son a place with a bathtub and a front yard to keep him quiet. And so Chandler was content with his newfound status at Stoke Ridge. It wasn't until recently that he realized just how much was in the bank account."

"How'd he find out?" The Beast asked.

"A very public lawsuit."

"A lawsuit?" The Beast replied.

"Yes. A lawsuit. Someone in New York realized Trent had a fake diploma on his wall. That's the real reason he didn't want his son to go to NC State: not only did Trent not get in there, he'd never even finished college. And we're talking Hampton Law, a Baptist school that believes religion's got something to do with it. In any case, when Trent was a student he had to drop out 'cause of an addiction to barbiturates, but his family was willing to pay up. They managed to buy him a diploma and a job at a pharmaceutical company . . . Sivistra or Sinvistra or something like that."

"What was the actual job?" The Beast asked.

"Clinical-trials-gone-wrong. Organ failures, respiratory problems, heart attacks, and the like. Trent counter-sued people who ended up sick or dead, but got himself in trouble when someone finally asked to see his credentials, hence the lawsuit and the attempted liquidation of Chandler's funds, and the resulting Chinatown bus to Canada that ended his life."

"I imagine he didn't leave much for his son," The Beast surmised.

"You'd be right on that front. Just a single letter. But a majority of the funds were still intact."

"What did the letter say?" Slim asked.

"It was from Sasha. She'd asked Trent to give it to Chandler on the day of her fateful jump. Trent didn't seem to think that was wise . . ."

"A suicide note?" Slim was intrigued.

"Not exactly. It said Chandler wouldn't have to worry about money anymore, that he was free to do what he wanted. That he should go to college. She said the jump was for him—that's why she chose the seventy-six-foot fall."

"Why seventy-six?" The Beast asked.

"She chose his birth year for the jump," I responded.

The Beast shook his head. "What a way to go out. How did he take it? When did he get the letter?"

"Just a few months ago. He didn't come here for weeks. But he seems calmer now, what with his father gone. The past few weeks have been okay. He's only talked about the letter once. Said he's moved on and that he's going to buy a house. That and a red Corvette—real original, right? But that's Dykes, is it not? Ever since his dad died he's been talking about how much money he has. The only other thing he's been talking about is trying to find Coach Brees—"

"Why does he want to find Coach Brees?" The Beast sat up.

"Learn more about the incident, I presume. He wants as much information on you as possible. Doesn't sound like Brees wants to talk to him, though. Dykes has been trying to get in touch with him for months, but I can't imagine Dykes is too good about reaching out. I went over to his place the day before yesterday to fix his television—that damned screeching opossum almost made me fall down. Just like the last time, there were whiskey bottles and pizza boxes strewn across the carpet. The place smelled like wet dog. Maybe wet opossum. But this time there wasn't anything on the walls. No pictures. No articles. He really did seem to be moving out. The place felt even emptier than before. Of course, the television didn't need fixing. It was just on the wrong input. One year of a static screen 'cause he thought the TV was wrong. And then yesterday he came in, really excited about something. Had a piece of paper in his pocket. 'This is it, Lockart.'"

"What was it?" The Beast asked.

"Can't say. But he said it was what he'd been waiting for all this time. Said it was thanks to your interview 'Meet the Prospects.'"

The Beast looked at Slim. "Fuck."

12

Meet the Prospects

Hugh Dawton-Fields, aka The Beast

"[…] and to thank you for coming on. So I have to ask Hugh, what made you agree to this interview? You've been dogged about your refusal to—"

"I wanted to clear the air, that's all. It's time for a new chapter, you know? Time to move on."

"Well we appreciate it, Hugh. So last year you thought you may never play again. And you said there was a possibility you wouldn't return for the fall?"

"Yeah, briefly. I needed a break from basketball. It was tough, you know, what with my parents and Coach Brees and all."

"Would you mind telling us a bit more about that?"

"Yeah, actually, I would."

"Okay, that's fair. No problem. So what made you decide to come back to college?"

"Well, again, it wasn't to return to college, but to play basketball. In some ways I didn't have a choice, but that's neither here nor there. It's not every day you get to compete for a championship."

"What do you mean, you didn't have a choice?"

"I misspoke. Never mind. I do love the game. I missed it. And I felt I owed it to my parents to finish college."

"Some say you lost your edge after junior year. Your passion, others call it. Your love for the game. I'm sure this isn't the first time you've heard it, but is there a grain of truth to that? I mean, you play a bit differently now ... a bit calmer, less aggressive?

"You must not have seen the ACC championship."

"The Jinson foul, right ... but that wasn't wholly your fault."

"Tell that to the NCAA. But maybe you're right. I did lose a certain edge, but I think that's a good thing. I don't think the passion is gone, just evolved. I was thankful for some time away—it helped me put some things in perspective. I love the game, sure. But I have a life outside of basketball."

"So it's not your first priority?"

"That's not what I said, not at all. I just think there comes a point when you realize what's most important to you in life."

"And what *is* most important to you?"

"Friendship. Family. Honesty and respect. That's why Slim is representing me as an agent."

"You've been fairly vocal about him in this interview—"

"Well yeah, he's important to me. Actually, he was the one who convinced me to do this interview, so you can thank Slim for that."

"So the question everyone wants to know: Why'd you decide to take him on as your agent? I mean, I get you two are close, but he's not exactly the obvious choice. Did he tell you something different? Something you weren't getting from the rest?"

"Well first, he's not my agent, not on paper anyway. I'm technically representing myself. But as far as telling me something different, that's exactly why I respect his opinion: he didn't *tell me* anything."

"What do you mean?"

"When you're making these decisions, you've got so many people telling you what you should do, what you shouldn't do ... it's hard to tell who really cares about you and who's in it for the wrong reasons. And sometimes you forget the best person to listen to is yourself. It's cliché maybe, but it's the truth. I mean, I don't exactly need an agent to get drafted. And there's so much money involved, endorsements and all the rest of it ... so Slim helped me see that it has to be my choice, not someone else's. And this is a business we're talking about. It *is* about the money. That's why I was wary about giving the reigns to somebody else—"

"Wary?"

"Wary about being manipulated."

"Manipulated by who?"

"By an agent, by a coach, by a company, a sponsor, whoever. At the end of the day I have to think about what's best for me. And now that my parents are gone, more than ever I have to be aware of that."

"But for a lottery pick not getting an agent...well it's a bit unorthodox, isn't it? What do you think about all the rumors? Do you think—"

"I stopped worrying about rumors when I got to high school."

"So you don't want to speak to them?"

"What's there to speak to?"

"Okay, that's fair. So where do you see yourself going? Top five? Top ten? Everyone's talking about Milwaukee. Ideally where would you like to play?"

"To be honest I'm not too concerned where I end up. Number one, number ten, number twenty, it doesn't matter. That's not for me to decide. All I can say is I'm excited for the next chapter. With everything that happened junior year, I'm ready to get on with my life and out of North Carolina."

"So you don't want to play for the Bobcats then?

"You're going to get me in trouble [*laughs*]."

"I'm sure Jordan understands. I know you're a big fan. So I've heard you've got your own opinions about the NCAA..."

"Well yeah. I am banned from playing for life, right? Not much else they can do to me. At least I have my degree. Look, you can guess how I feel about it: it's a business, plain and simple. Us athletes aren't as dumb as you may think. They owe it to us to treat us more like human beings instead of property. College athletes entertain millions. They bring in hundreds of millions of dollars a year. Doesn't that sound like a group of people who deserve to get paid?"

"Well you do get scholarships ..."

"[*Laughs*] We're talking about state-school tuition. What is that, eight grand? Do you know how much the athletic director gets paid? Over five hundred thousand dollars in salary alone. His bonus is five times the cost of in-state tuition. Don't talk to me about scholarship; you and I both know it's a joke. [*Hesitates*] Slim has told me to hold my tongue on this, but since it's my first interview I might as well be honest. Being an NCAA athlete is indentured servitude. Look up the definition before you scoff. They used to have their tickets paid for to go to the New World; they were given room and board in exchange for contracted years of service. Most came from the lower ranks of society, hoping to better themselves with promises of freedom. If you work hard, their masters said, one day it will pay off. Extortion isn't illegal if you draw up a contract. Good business in the NCAA is just ritualized thievery."

"Wow. Okay. That's a bold claim. So if NCAA athletes are indentured servants, what's the alternative?"

"It's simple: pay the athletes a percentage of the profits. There's no reason good business and fair business have to be mutually exclusive, especially when you see how much money our coaches make. My lasting legacy at UNC will be a couple of mansions on East Franklin Street. I mean, I've made more money for the school than last year's graduating class combined. So who is giving who the opportunity, really?"

"So how much should you get paid?"

"For starters we should get a percentage of ticket sales and TV contracts. Look, I'm not a businessman. And that's the problem with us athletes: they know most of us will never think about profit. You know, during March Madness alone hundreds of millions of dollars go into the NCAA coffers. The only reason I'm not already a professional is because I don't get paid. But the only way to make a change would be for some kind of sit-in like

Woolworth's. You'd need a decent amount of the top players in the country to refuse to play the games. I mean, can you imagine the players at Duke or UNC saying they wouldn't play until they got paid? But what kind of player is going to do that? What eighteen-year-old kid with a supposed future in the NBA is going to start *that* conversation? We're teenagers. We're swayed by free shoes and free meals. Until the guys at the top realize they have to pay the kids who make them rich, until they're held accountable for the futures of those who never make it professionally, nothing will change. There's too much money involved for them to go down without a famous player making a major political statement. And no, this interview won't help. At best it will start an online conversation. You talk about idealism . . . can you imagine a day when money wasn't everything? When we watched and played the game for the only reason that matters?"

"Is it really that simple?"

"How could it be any more complicated? You think Kobe or LeBron keep going out there to buy an extra Mercedes? That's one thing you guys don't realize . . . the effort it takes to play. And I'm not talking about the physical effort as much as the emotional one. You have to live and breathe the game. You can't afford to take a day off. Self-discipline is the most important and most invisible human trait."

"Okay, but that's hypothetical. If you believe in all of this, why did you keep playing the game? Why *didn't* you take a stand? Why did you decide to play?"

"Like I said, UNC made it worthwhile. It wasn't just basketball, I wanted the degree."

"So are you saying you're still questioning a move to the NBA?"

"I'm not saying anything. You're a journalist. Spin it in your own way. UNC didn't support me at all. Now that I'm banned I can say it. I lost them millions because of Coach Brees. They told me directly. They said I had an obligation to play. So of course that made me think about why I was playing the game. Just to make them money? No. I wanted to play because I love the game. And they harassed me that summer. A certain someone, every day."

"Was that certain someone Coach Brees, by chance?"

"Does it really matter? What I'm saying is it wasn't the Health and Wellness center making sure I was alright. I knew why the phone was ringing. But I got a degree—that was part of the goal. I didn't want them to take my passion away from me."

"And did they?"

"[Hesitates] I don't think so. Not yet anyway."

"Okay, final question. What will be your legacy? What do you want to be remembered for at UNC?"

"For something other than Coach Brees and my parents' deaths. You know my dad always said that we're like sculptures—when something bad happens it cracks you, fragments break off inevitably. But he always said what mattered was what's on the inside. Do the cracks let the light in? Or does the darkness seep out?"

* * *

"What with my parents and the Jim Brees Incident, the conspiracy theories got out of control. That's also why I wanted to do the interview," The Beast said. "One columnist said I was a schizophrenic and that I'd been institutionalized—I didn't leave for the NBA senior year because my doctors wouldn't allow it. Another wrote about my parents, tried to dig up some dirt . . . said they couldn't pay their debts and so someone started the fire. As for Jim Brees, they had a field day with that. One journalist said he'd been secretly abusing me . . . another said we were lovers. Some said he caused the fire, others said I held a grudge . . . or that the coaching staff wanted me gone . . . it went on and on and on. The most interesting theory was that the NCAA was behind it . . . that they forced me away from the spotlight to protect their image because they knew I'd speak out against student-athlete policies. It's true: I'd already spoken to coaches about the possibility of starting a union, and they didn't want their star player speaking out. It was good journalism to the extent that it brought to light the larger issue, but still, everything about the incident was speculation."

"And the truth?"

"The truth is I didn't like Coach Brees at all. He harassed me for months after the fire, waiting outside my house, banging on the front door, threatening me if I didn't come back to the team, saying I was losing him and the program money and that if I really wanted to honor my parents I should stop being such a sissy. Still, I wasn't planning to punch him and obviously didn't mean to put him into a coma. But when I got back in the gym and saw him for the first time, my blood was already simmering; and then he made it boil. I didn't mean to punch him that hard, but he pushed me too far . . ."

"Why didn't you say that in the interview?" I asked.

"Legal reasons," The Beast paused and shifted on his stool. "I don't want to talk about it. The point is, I did the interview to let the people decide. I'm sure Dykes will interpret it as he wants. Coach Brees too, he's already tried to contact me twice. But I'm done with all of that."

The Beast became reticent. "He won't stop until he sees me fall . . ."

"Oh shit, not this again." Slim took a swig of whiskey. "Hugh's got this theory, see? Just like the rest of 'em. He thinks Coach Brees has some vendetta against him."

"It's not a theory, Slim . . . you don't understand—"

"Oh I understand plain and simple: you're afraid he's gonna get back at you. I can understand it . . . I mean, how does flipping burgers count as just punishment? I'm sure he had medical bills to pay, too. But the judge liked you, right? He loved your parents' restaurant. So Coach Brees stays sour. Big deal. No problem."

The Beast's breath was shallow, as if he were afraid to let it out. For a moment it seemed Hugh was about to respond. The words lingered on his lips. They began to slip out of his mouth. "Slim . . . there's something with the contract I haven't told you about."

"Contract? Oh come on, Hugh. We've already talked about this."

"No, it's not—"

"I know exactly what it is, Hugh. Listen to this, Lockart. Hugh's afraid that maybe he isn't meant to be a ballplayer. He refused to let me sign as his agent in case he backs out."

"Slim, that's not what I'm talking—"

"Come on, Hugh, you gotta stop it. He keeps thinking if he goes to Milwaukee he'll go down the wrong path."

The Beast sighed and shook his head. Slim took his silence for confirmation.

"You know I'm right, Hugh. You've got cold feet. That's all."

"It isn't cold feet—"

"You think it's just some accident you're so good at basketball? You were born to play the game . . . you're seven feet tall for fuck's sake! We've talked about this before—are you going to flip burgers all your life? You've spent your whole life getting to this point—you're going to give up now?"

The Beast's tone was more aggressive. "Have I really worked that hard, Slim? What exactly did I do to be seven feet tall?"

"You know that's not what I'm saying, man. Imagine not knowing what you want to do when you get up in the morning. I'd kill to be in your position. You're just jaded, that's all. Imagine the opposite problem—no choice at all. I can't even imagine having an option. So don't talk to me about wrong choices again—at least you have decisions to make. Do you know what that's like, not having anything to go on? It's like there's this hall full of flies, thousands of 'em flying around, and there's exactly one with a red dot on its back and I'm supposed to find it."

"You took that from Harry Potter," The Beast replied. "The room with the flying keys."

"I didn't take it from Harry Potter. They're flies and it's a hall. Plus Harry finds the right key, right? Do you see any keys in my pocket? I start getting anxious 'cause I'm scared I'll never find it and . . . well, it's like I don't know the next chapter in my own novel. Do I have to tell you again? *At least you have a decision to make.* You keep talking about the NBA like it's a hard decision. Are you really going to pass up that kind of opportunity 'cause you feel conflicted about it? Isn't that part of being an adult, choosing between two options, neither of which you're really confident about? Well, at least you're in that predicament. I still don't know what I want to be when I grow up—"

The doorbell jingled. Cool air rushed into the bar. Slim and The Beast stood up instinctively, their chests puffed out, alarmed.

"I thought you'd be coming by. Why'd you bring the pickup?" I stood up.

My wife Jane smiled and took off her raincoat, swiping off the water before entering, hanging her raincoat on the wall.

"Storms a comin'. That must be your boys' Jeep out there? Nice to see someone other than the sergeant in the bar!" Jane craned her head when she shook hands with Slim and The Beast.

"It's a pleasure," Jane said. "Nice to meet you, Slim. As for you, Hugh, well I know who you are. You know I used to go to Chez Moi?

Even met your parents a couple of times. Nice folks, a real tragedy. But knowing your parents, they're smiling down on you right now. Best food in the state in my opinion. Ever thought about re-opening it? I heard a rumor you're quite the cook yourself," she ended with a smile.

"Pleasure to meet you too, ma'am—"

"And polite, too! But there's no need for formalities around these parts. Call me Jane, it's less awkward—ma'am is for old ladies with Southern drawls, hierarchies, and all the rest of it. Excuse me for interrupting, looks like you boys were in quite the conversation. But see my husband here—I prefer to call him Carl—well, he's fixing to be put out on account of the storm."

"Put out? How's that?" I was instinctively pouring Jane a Jameson. She told Slim to scooch and sat between the two of 'em. "Cheaper than Redbreast, but I like it somehow. Sitting between these two makes me feel like I've got bodyguards! Are you two staying the night? Don't worry about your slumber party, I won't be staying long."

The Beast looked at Slim. "We weren't planning on it . . . but it's a thought."

"Well, I can tell you," Jane sipped her whiskey. "It better be more than just a thought! You'll have to excuse my husband . . . he tends to forget about the world outside. This is his own little sanctuary, you know? And I'm thankful for it, too. But you've gotta look out the window from time to time, Carl. What are two young men like you doing in a country bar? Starting to rain mighty hard out there. You might end up getting stuck!"

"We're heading up to the draft," Slim replied.

"And you stopped at a country bar during a hurricane? You know I-40's already flooding . . ."

Neither had an answer.

"They wanted to try a burger," I said. "Seems like a rumor's been going around . . ."

"Food being served at Lockart's? Well, I've heard just about everything now! Well, you boys will stay the night . . . isn't safe to be driving now. All holed up in a bar, isn't that something. Carl, when'd you put the painting up?" Jane sipped her whiskey and walked over to *Nighthawks*.

"Just a few days ago. Got it framed and all."

"That you did," Jane said. "And it's about time! He knows it's one of my favorites . . . me and the rest of the country, right? But there's something to it, isn't there? Why it's so popular? That's what I learned in Chicago . . . some types of beauty transcend the confines of life."

"Jane was an art history major . . . liable to talk your head off!"

Jane laughed. "If you can't speak freely about what you love, well then what *can* you talk about?" Jane raised her glass. "I order the same thing every time: Jameson on the rocks. Anyhow, this painting: you see how the light touches all the objects?" Slim and The Beast walked over to the wall.

"Edward Hopper," Jane said. "I used to stand in front of it for hours. Not looking, but watching—that's the difference with good art. See the light pouring out into the darkness? How they seem to be hiding from something in the night? I tried to find the place once. Inspired by a restaurant where two streets meet, Hopper said. Well, as you can imagine, I never found it. It doesn't exist anymore. Maybe it never did. But does it matter? It still exists on this wall. Portraying the reality of a place that no longer exists—that's the beauty, in my opinion, anyhow. What do you boys think? Noticing anything else going on?"

"That one man has no face . . . seems like a stranger in the diner," Slim said.

"Well, you can't see his face, you're right. Who knows what he looks like."

"The man and the woman don't seem to know each other either," The Beast said. "Definitely looks like they're hiding out."

The Beast peered into the painting. "There's no entrance. There's a door to another room, but how do they get out?"

"I didn't think you'd catch that!" Jane said. "You've got quite the eye. No exit, you're right. Unless they jump through those windows, of course. Speaking of windows, how *exactly* were you planning to board 'em up, Carl? I know for a fact there ain't no plywood around these parts."

"There's still some wood out by the shed. And there should be nails behind the bar." Like a scolded child I looked in the drawers even though I knew it was futile.

Jane put her hands on Slim and The Beast's backs. "Don't take his word for it—I used the wood and the nails last week for a new sculpture. I swear, sometimes I wonder why I married the man at all! But that's not true, I know why. Plywood and nails behind the bar . . ." Jane laughed. "Can't very well stop a hurricane without any plywood. You know the wind's gonna be over one hundred and fifty miles per hour? Listen, you two boys, why don't you go outside and bring in those boards from the back of my truck? I heard the screen door creak when I walked in. I thought you were gonna fix it honey . . ."

"Well I did fix it, but when they came in—"

"You know how I feel about excuses . . . only satisfy those who make 'em. Run out back to get the nails for the plywood. I'll fix that hinge right now. As for you two, could you grab the wood? It isn't raining too hard."

Slim and The Beast gathered the wood from the back of Jane's truck as I went to look in the wood shed for a couple of hammers and nails. Slim and The Beast and I spent the next ten minutes boarding up the bay windows in the front; by the time we were finished, the

screen door didn't creak anymore. Jane was standing on the front
porch, glass of water in hand. Her long gray hair cascaded over her
shoulders. "Well, I've got to get going. Research for my new sculpture.
Trying to reflect light through multiple prisms à la Hopper. Carl, you
be wise with the whiskey . . . reminds me of your old Boys' Nights!
If you need something you call on the walkie-talkie—I left it on the
kitchen counter. I trust Dykes isn't coming in today? You said he's
afraid of the storm, anyhow. I'll see you boys in the morning then.
If I'm feeling kind I'll bring some tea. Carl, I'll be downstairs in the
living room with my books, candles alight."

Jane bade farewell. I accompanied her to the door. I held out her
raincoat. She slid in her arms.

"Better to be a gentleman than a handyman, anyhow." She smiled
at Slim and The Beast. "Enjoy the evening and don't fret about staying the night!"

Jane scampered to the pickup and peeled out in a wake of mud.

We returned to the bar. "What's this about Dykes being afraid of
the storm?" The Beast asked.

"She's right," Slim replied. "He always was afraid of the rain.
Anytime there was a thunderstorm he'd make us stay late and work
out. Always with the rain, pattering on the roof, just like it is right
now. There was this one night in his office. First time he forced me
to stay the night. It was at the workout with the rest of the boys. I
couldn't get past four hundred pushups. He just smiled and looked
at me, egging me on. It was pattering outside. My arms were dead
weight, you know? He picked me up like a limp dog and told me to
get on the line. That was the rule: if you couldn't do pushups, you
had to run suicides. But that particular night I told him I wasn't gonna
do it. I said he was going to have to carry me if he wanted me to get
to the other baseline. That's when he told everyone else to leave and

took me back to his office. Then he got all paternal and caring, right? Once I was indoors. After hours of screaming and yelling, after I'd tried to resist, I was exhausted; well, once I was exhausted, he'd take me into his arms. I was still young then, still skinny. He could pick me up no problem. I didn't like it, but what was I gonna do? I was a kid. So he'd scoop me up off the floor and say I could sleep under his desk. He was obsessed with it . . . always made me stay under it. Now I know where the impulse came from."

Slim swigged his whiskey. "I know what you're thinking, but Dykes never made me blow him, all right? He did some fucked up things, but . . . well anyway, it doesn't matter. I don't want to go into it—aren't shirtless pushups in his office and sleeping on his floor enough? Most nights I woke up with a puddle of drool on the carpet, around three or four in the morning, when everything's quiet, when you think you've got the silence for yourself. But he was always awake, watching. Staring at me all quiet—his hairy legs (he always wore khaki shorts) under the desk and his face in the lamplight. He wasn't doing anything, just staring down at the floor, stroking the stuffed opossum, rocking back and forth in his chair. He always had a plaid pillow in his lap. Sometimes he'd lie down on the carpet next to me when he thought I was sleeping. I knew it was strange and always felt dirty in the morning, like *I'd* done something wrong, not wholly unlike the feeling after a one-night stand. But I was weak back then. I wasn't used to the workouts. I remember watching the light fade as we walked to his office."

"So what made you stop?" The Beast asked.

"I got used to working out. He didn't think I'd ever get strong enough. And then there was this one time, a prelude to a coming storm. I knew he'd hit me when I refused to run the suicides—just three days prior I'd seen him break another kid's nose—but something changed when I refused. I realized I had a choice. For the first time I sensed fear."

"Did he beat you?"

"Well, first he said I lied about how many pushups I'd done and that everyone had to run suicides because of it. He tried to turn everyone else against me, but I said he wasn't going to take me back to his office that night. All of a sudden the other cadets got quiet 'cause they didn't know what I was talking about. Dykes didn't know what to say, and his face got all red. He started scratching his neck—you've probably seen it, Lockart—like he's got some rash around his Adam's apple. And so he started yelling about respect and obeying orders and what not . . . typical military bullshit." Slim sipped his whiskey. "And then, yeah, he beat the shit out of me— concussion and a broken rib and all the rest of it. But I didn't cry about it. I didn't react. And from that point on I knew I'd figured him out: he couldn't stand the idea of not controlling me 'cause that meant he had to control himself. He wanted to teach me strength without letting me be strong—the very thing that made me attached to him became the reason for moving on. Discipline will do that to you—why do you think dictators are so powerful at first? But after a few years, respect turned into dissent. I no longer trusted him; I didn't revere him. I realized he was the one who was weak. I don't remember if there was a storm the night the real change went down, but I know it was raining, always the patter on the rooftop. Dykes was sitting on the bleachers with one of those thin, cheap sweatshirts and khaki shorts on, wearing that yellow-hued Titleist hat, screaming his lungs out.

"Dykes yelled at me from across the hardwood, getting up in a hurry, loping over from his seat. 'Boy!' Dykes came at me. 'Get down and give me a hundred! What are you, a faggot? Ten suicides, the whole team!'

"The cadets lined up on the baseline," Slim said. Dykes prepared to blow the whistle.

A lankier version of Slim stepped out of line. "Fuck you, Dykes. I'm done. It's two a.m."

"What'd you say?" Dykes was stunned.

"I said fuck you, sergeant. I'm not doing it. You're gonna have to make me. Me and the rest of the team."

Slim's peers shuffled nervously. Although red-faced, Dykes managed a snigger. "You don't know when to quit, do you boy? Now I'm going to have to teach you a lesson . . ."

Dykes descended on Slim as if he were a dog, grabbing the back of Slim's neck, squeezing the flesh of the nape. "Drop down and give me *two hundred*. Do it now, boy, if you know what's good for you."

Slim, prostrate, placed his forearms on the ground and squirmed away. He stood up, raised his arms, and squared off, ready to fight. "Let's do it then. Let's go. Can't take me back to your office, can you Dykes? Lay your hands on me, see what happens. Hey boys, watch this. I'm about to fuck the sergeant up!"

Dykes tried again for Slim's neck. Slim evaded his grasp. When Slim pushed Dykes's chest, the sergeant tried to grab hold of Slim's wrists. But Slim pushed outward, resisting with all of his strength, once again showing that he wouldn't back down. "See that Dykes? You don't have shit."

Dykes ripped his hand away from Slim in horror. He puffed his chest out but was clearly shaken. "You're going to wish you—"

"Now you listen here, Dykes," Slim pointed his finger in Dykes's face. "And you listen good. Stop calling me son. I'm not your boy and I'm not your nephew. I'm not a goddamn child. Now I'm gonna give you to the count of three to get out of my face before I break your teeth and scatter them across the hardwood. You're a cunt, plain and simple. One, two, th—"

Slim cocked his right fist back and swung. Dykes ducked. Slim missed. But Slim's left hook landed square in the sergeant's gut. Dykes stumbled backwards. For a moment he stood in awe. It was the first time he'd been touched, let alone punched, in over a decade. But he soon regained his footing and came back in force. Dykes grabbed Slim's neck and slammed him to the ground. Slim's nose exploded. The sergeant bashed Slim's face into the foul line before placing his knee in the nape of Slim's neck. Slim's cheekbone cracked. At least one tooth was lost. "You're going to stay down and give me *three hundred*, SON. And you'll take your shirt off while you're at it. Now the rest of you boys watch: you're about to learn a valuable lesson in respect."

Dykes ripped Slim's shirt down the middle of the back. Slim's muscles went limp. As Dykes tried to beat a response out of the cadet, his prodigy lay prostrate on the hardwood, barely making a sound.

"You're losing it, Dykes," Slim spluttered and laughed. "You're done, Dykes, you're done!" Dykes slowed down his pace. He couldn't believe what he was hearing.

"Look at this boys—Dykes still thinks he's in control!" As the sergeant repeatedly slammed Slim's face into the hardwood, the cadets watched, stupefied, as the court turned magenta. Blood flowed freely from a deep gash in Slim's upper lip. Though he still had oxygen, his face was turning blue. There was a moment of respite as Dykes wheezed and caught his breath.

"Come on, Dykes, go on," Slim spit out a gob of blood and raised himself up on an elbow. "You're working overtime, these aren't school hours. Everyone's seen it now. I'm not afraid of you anymore, you cunt."

Slim began to crawl on elbows toward half-court. Dykes rested for a moment, his hands on his knees, breathing heavily. It seemed he'd had enough.

Slim propped himself up and managed to get to his feet. "Is that all you've got, you miserable fuck? I always knew you were weak." Dykes looked up. "See, I'm not like you, Dykes. I'll always be better off. And you know why? 'Cause I can take it. These scars will heal. I can take the beatings, no problem. And I'll forget you, too. But you? No way. You're gonna die in that sad little office."

Dykes started to mutter under his breath, keeping his eyes on Slim.

"Hey boys? You hear this? He's talking to himself now! Listen real good, Dykes: I'm gonna ruin your goddamned life. You hear me, sergeant? How does it feel to be so goddamn alone?"

Dykes's eyes darted around the gym, past the shocked expressions of the other boys. Then the sergeant walked over to Slim, brought him to the ground in one punch, turned him over on his stomach, and put his knee in Slim's back. Slim laughed. Dykes moaned. He got down on both knees, straddling Slim on the floor. Dykes lowered himself down to a pushup stance, bringing his lips close to Slim's ear. The sergeant quivered above Slim's body as if he were about to enter him. He whispered so only Slim could hear. "One more word and you're gonna wish you never left that shithole shack where your mother forgot to raise you. I should've fucked her two more times and left you in the creek where you belonged. She couldn't even speak by the time I was done with her."

"My eyes started flickering," Slim recounted at the bar. "Somewhere inside I could feel a low hum. My vision blurred, you know? And my hearing got all fuzzy. Like I was wearing headphones or on drugs. But I didn't want Dykes to think he'd gotten to me."

Once Dykes stood up, Slim propped himself up on one arm, using the other hand to check the blood seeping from his mouth. The gash was flowing. A cheekbone was shattered. He could only see out of one eye. Dykes spat on the ground and returned to the bleachers. His sweatshirt was bloodied. He ran a crimson hand across his skull and through his receding hairline. But as soon as he yelled at the cadets to hit the showers, a cackling laughter proved him wrong. "And what about your mom, Dykes?" Slim said between bloodied spits. "How come she never comes around?"

Slim stood up. "How come during family weekends you've never had a visitor? How come everyone knows you're depressed and alone?"

Dykes turned around.

"You know what I think?" Slim continued. "I think I know you, Dykes. I think I know you better than you know yourself. And I think you should give up. Look at you, sitting there on the bleachers. You just beat up a teenager. Are you proud? You think that makes you strong? You watch us work out with our shirts off. You make me sleep in your office."

Slim shook his head as he neared the end of his story. The Beast remained silent. "Well, as you can imagine, he went ape shit. See this scar?" Slim pointed to a white line above his eyebrow. "Fractured orbital part of the frontal bone. Had to have surgery. Could've gone blind. I knew when he started charging that I was in for a rough ride . . ."

The cadets sprinted to Slim's aid, but in some ways it was too late—the sergeant was already slamming Slim's entire body into the hardwood. Slim's nose exploded once again. "If he'd slammed my head even one more time, the doctor said, my skull would've been crushed. The only reason he didn't break my back was 'cause of all the muscles." As the puddle of blood spread toward the three-point line, the rest of the cadets piled atop Dykes. He writhed underneath, trying to get back to Slim. After five minutes of flailing, the cadets managed to restrain Dykes, but not before he'd crushed Slim's nose, fractured his cheekbone and collarbones, caused a severe concussion, broken three ribs, cracked four teeth, and sent four muscular cadets to the hospital. In a meeting with General Haith the following day, Dykes explained how there had been a brawl. He had tried to stop it, and that's why he too was injured; "no one was willing to rat on him," Slim said. "He outright said he'd kill anyone who talked. But I knew that's what he wanted . . . for someone to rat on him. It killed him that everyone just wanted to move on. And what was I gonna do? File charges and go home? I knew Dykes would keep coming—he's crazy like that. Now sure I got fucked up, but from that day forward I was in complete control. I knew he was scared. He expected all of us to rat on him, but he'd trained us too well. Why buy into the fear when we could use it to control him? There's nothing easier for a teenager to learn than revenge. Some cadets left Stoke Ridge, but I kept working out. I took pleasure in defying him. The bigger I got, the more angry he became—all of it came to a head at the award ceremony, as you know, and if it weren't for General Haith, I'd be dead right now. It's a shame I couldn't see him one more time. He was the only one who ever scared Dykes . . . and now, as usual, Dykes is still my problem."

"I'll go out and on check on him," I interrupted.

"Didn't you say he's afraid of Beverly?" The Beast replied.

"Just to be sure. I'll check out his cabin, and then we'll get to cooking before the power goes out? The wind's already rattling. I'll just have one last cigarette before I lock up the place for the night."

13

I picked up a pair of binoculars on the back porch. Dykes's cabin was camouflaged in the forest's shadows. The entire tree line swayed high above, submitting to the rain and the heavy winds.

As I peered at the scene, I couldn't see any glare from the TV—there were wooden boards stacked up on the side of his cabin, but none of the windows were protected from Hurricane Beverly. His convertible was there, which meant Dykes was in. Maybe he was in the bathtub, soaking like a prune; or maybe he was drunk, talking to Larry the Opossum. Thunder rumbled and cracked, shaking the foundations of the bar. The rain came in heaps and hit the porch diagonally. Tree branches started to crack—a wind-chime Jane built took a hit. I sprinted across the sodden ground, almost slipping in the mud, pausing under the canopy of the forest edge to untangle the strings and recover the sculpture.

"Catharsis?" Slim said when I came back indoors. I placed the wind chimes in the sink and turned on the faucet before putting on Miles Davis's *Kind of Blue.*

"Right. And it could be God, or many gods, whatever," The Beast said.

"Glass of water?" I asked.

"Sure, why not. And you might not be religious, but you've still gotta respect it, Slim. You don't have to agree to respect their effort . . ."

"But that's why you get people like Dykes," Slim disagreed with his friend. "All the extremists. What's this obsession with always having to listen to everybody, anyway? I always hated anthropology."

"But can't you see the problem with that?" The Beast said. "You think you're better off *not knowing* what makes Sergeant Dykes tick? Excluding people's opinions never works out in the long run. Just because Dykes is crazy doesn't mean you shouldn't understand him. Maybe it means you should understand him all the more. The problem is he thinks he's right, but you think you're right, too. No, of course not. Of course he's not right. But when it's all said and done, that's not the point, is it?"

"Yeah, yeah, okay. Recognize that it's all subjective, anthropology, blah, blah, blah. But is it? I don't know. You don't have to be right for some people to be wrong, do you? I mean, I'll listen to those people looking for the truth but not the ones with a preconceived answer before they even begin the search."

"Well, Dykes is still trying to find out more about me and you . . . so according to you he's seeking truth?"

"Well no . . . that's what I'm saying. Dykes is only searching for answers to support his theory."

"And what theory is that?" I asked.

"Lord if I know," Slim replied. "But he isn't trying to find answers to better understand. And that's the problem, isn't it? I mean, you wonder why we've got so many problems in the world. The people who think they've got the answer . . . they can't help but relate everything to it."

"Well that's the point of faith right?" The Beast suggested. "To believe in something without proof? But still, come on Slim, does that mean it's worthless?"

"No, faith is necessary. That's what got me here . . . well, part of the way anyway. But if I've got faith, and you've got it, and Lockart's got it too, well then we are all entitled to our own personal version. The problem with Dykes is he's always trying to convince others 'cause he's not confident in his own opinion. And that's the worst kind of religiosity, right? Convincing people that *your version* is the truth? No, the way I see it, claiming answers is desecrating something. It's the easy way out. The whole point is it gets us questioning so we can question and then cultivate ourselves."

"That was Voltaire, right? Or was it Rousseau?"

"Voltaire. *Candide*. But see the problem is Dykes thinks he's right 'cause he's the loudest guy in the bar. But he's scared of asking the questions, the ones he's afraid to answer. And the reason he tries so hard to believe in his own cause is 'cause deep down he's not sure at all. He's got no faith in himself, so he tries to put it somewhere else. That's why he was so obsessed with Dykes's Tykes—the paradox being he made me realize the futility of searching for meaning in others."

Slim paused for a moment as if he were unsure of what he'd said. "If you don't have faith in yourself, well, how are you supposed to have faith in something else, right? That's why I'm thankful for my first years at UNC . . . You know, when I first got there, I even considered going to church!"

"What's wrong with that?" The Beast asked.

"Man, there's no way a dude wearing a white robe serving you

crackers and red wine has the answer. Or a dude with a long beard
tying a black rope around your head and your arm. Or telling me
I've got to slit a goat's neck 'cause it's sacred or something. I mean
what are we talking about here? Really, what are we talking about?
We're talking about people who actually believe they can survive their
own death, putting happiness into someone else's hands, that God can
explain killing, that everything happens for a reason."

"You don't think everything happens for a reason?" The Beast
interjected.

"Well hold on now, Hugh, let me finish! I was about to say things
happen for a reason 'cause you can find a reason in everything. Lord
knows Dykes has been looking for one for years. But just 'cause you
can find a reason doesn't mean it actually exists. Alive in its questions,
religion dies in its answers. And that's the point of a horizon, right?
It's constantly receding. I mean, you know this Hugh, I don't need
to tell you twice. They're making a documentary about you based on
what? On an article someone wrote three years ago? Dykes is collecting
shitty newspaper articles as if they held some truth about you? All
this obsession with written words as if they made it canon . . . I don't
get it. Really, I don't. Like Nietzsche said, look the other way. I mean,
talk about lost in translation—Dykes doesn't have a clue about who
you are. But he's convinced that he does, and why? 'Cause he wants
to be convinced of something, that's all." Thunder cracked. "And so
now we've got some schizophrenic thinking he's a prophet and that
he's destined to find us. That's the real problem: he can't move on.
And he still comes in here and thinks it's profound. But maybe that's
just humanity, right? Delusion in the face of grandeur."

"I like that. *Delusion in the face of grandeur.*"

"I'm sure I heard it somewhere else. I don't state any claim to it.

Bottom line is it's okay to believe in something so long as we accept that it's also batshit crazy."

"Is that possible, though? To believe in something you admit is probably wrong?"

"Of course it's possible! We do it all the time. Even atheists say a prayer when the plane's going down . . ."

"So atheism is a better choice?"

"Better? Of course not. No better or worse. I mean, if there were a god, right? Let's assume a supreme being. Do you think It gives a shit about what we're thinking? We can't know It. It's unknowable. That's why we invented faith. You know, I used to have an intellectual hard-on for Richard Dawkins, but that guy's missing the point, too. See, atheists are just as convinced that they've got the answer. They're equally delusional in the face of grandeur. And you know what really grinds my gears? They've got this smug pretentious air about 'em like they're talking down to fifth-graders, as if they've surpassed some threshold of knowledge and have seen the light. But it's still ignorance. Agnosticism, that's the truth. It's the only rational choice. And if Neil deGrasse Tyson is down with it, well so can you."

"Ah, but see what you just did? Now *you're* proselytizing!" The Beast pointed out.

"No! And that's the point: agnosticism means we don't have the answer and maybe that we can't know it. And if you want to argue semantics and say that's an answer too, well then, yeah, the answer is we can't know. But maybe you've got a point in that I am convinced I'm right. That's part of being human, though . . . can't remain subjective all our life."

"But isn't that the problem?" The Beast asked. "That Dykes is equally convinced he's right? I mean, sometimes I think I've already found the answer, sometimes not. I guess that's the challenge of becoming an adult, though: making a decision to go down a certain path. Up until now I've always thought doubt was the most important thing, but maybe doubt can also force you to choose the wrong answer . . ."

"Are you telling me you think the NBA is the wrong path?"

"Did I say that? No. But sometimes I do get scared that I'll succeed in basketball and it will be nothing more than a profession."

"Well shit," Slim said. "Making a couple of million dollars a year playing a game you love sounds okay to me. I'm scared at a baseline level. I can't even consider making a decision. The more I study philosophy the more I just want a nice couch, a house, and a dog."

"Yeah, but we're young, Slim, you don't know what you—"

"We're not that young, Hugh. We're old enough to make a decision, anyway. *Old enough to repaint, young enough to sell.* Maybe not there, not yet, but you get the point. I'm sick of being transient. I want to create a life for myself. And even if that means a steady job and a nice girlfriend . . . well why is that so bad?"

"Who said it was bad? It's just not what I want, not right now."

"Speak for yourself, Hugh. I could use a cup of tea with a nice gal. And sometimes I get scared that I'll never have it, and that I'll never find out exactly what I want 'cause I'll spend all my time ruminating about the options until it's too late to be anything but a lonely hack of a philosopher. But it's hard to move on when you don't know where you're going . . . You know, I think about my days playing down at the creek, senior year together, even fighting in Iraq, and all those times where I felt connected that have passed, and then it hits me that they'll never happen again and all of that's gone. And I miss the way the leaves crunched under my feet when I was a kid. And I miss the way we used to talk and eat burgers at The Skillet. And I miss the way my mom would always fall asleep on the couch and how her hand would slide off and hang down to the side. And I can see it all, of course, but that's not the same thing as living it. And then I feel like an asshole 'cause I get all philosophical, and I get lonely 'cause I feel like all that's passed, and then I get depressed and, well shit, then I end up here, at the bar, like in that painting, hiding out."

"What do you think, Lockart?" The Beast asked.

"Well as far as I can tell," I pondered, "you're doing the right thing by asking the questions. The older guy at the bar *believes he's got the answer*. You're just considering it a possibility, not a fact. You're willing to accept an alternative, right?"

"Am I?" Slim wondered. "I don't know, Lockart. What have I seen in my life? I've seen Dykes turn out to be some kind of psychopath and Stoke Ridge to be the worst kind of family. I've seen the best years of my life packed up into a car. And I went to war 'cause I wanted to find meaning, and it worked for a time, but that's just 'cause I had a shitty past. But that's changing now, and maybe that's why I'm scared . . . You know sometimes I spend hours lying in bed trying to find a reason to get up? I wake up and stare at the ceiling literally for hours. And I think about what reason would get me out of bed; and I start philosophizing about why I can't find something worthy to get me out of bed, and then I start thinking I'm an idiot for philosophizing about it instead of just getting up and making eggs, all the while still lying in bed like a jackass."

"That's not just you, Slim. That's part of being human," The Beast replied. "You keep thinking I'm better off because I have a decision to make, but that's equally terrifying."

"Well," Slim said, "if you want to change spots, be my guest. You've got a guaranteed contract. You know, studying social theory and postulating about existence is easy 'cause I find comfort in asking the questions. But maybe philosophizing is just a cop-out 'cause I'm afraid to live out the answers. And maybe all those hours spent in the books, well, maybe they're just an excuse to avoid confronting the cause. It's like Hemingway said, maybe I don't care what it's all about . . . maybe I just want to figure out a way to live in it. And maybe that's the only way to learn—to experience life. 'Cause the only time I've ever felt alive was out there on the battlefield, and even that was just a palliative fix 'cause when you're out there you *have* to live in the moment or you'll die. And if I'm really being honest? I feel most alive talking with you, Hugh. Doing exactly this, postulating. *This* makes me feel alive. And so yeah, I'm scared of the future. I'm scared it's just a matter of time. And I'm afraid that things won't work out and that the first time something really bad happens to me I'm going to break down, just like Dykes. I mean, I've experienced some pain, but come on, not really. A couple scars here and there. Nothing profound. And so I've got all these high and mighty opinions about myself and about seeking truth, but have I been challenged to really apply them? No. I'm just a theorist, that's all. And I'm lazy 'cause I've got weed and whiskey and an Xbox. In the moment it makes me happy, but not in the long run. But then again, maybe the moment's all we've got. So every day is a battle to feel like I can connect, and maybe that's why it's taken me so long to realize that asking the questions without a willingness to confront the answers doesn't mean shit."

There was a moment of silence—not awkward, but quiet. The rain pattered on the roof. The windows rattled in the wind. Miles Davis's "All Blues" filled the bar.

"Slim, I have to tell you someth—"

"Just one second," Slim cut his friend off. "I'm just about finished. You know, hanging with you has been the best part of my life. Solitude versus loneliness, you know? We've talked about that. But here we are, driving toward Milwaukee."

"That's what I wanted to—"

"And I know I've gotta move on. I can't live your life. But—"

"Slim," The Beast cut in. "That's what I wanted to—"

"Hold up, let me finish. If there's one thing I've learned about becoming some kind of adult it's that you have to make decisions you aren't sure will pan out. Making a decision that's only fifty-one percent sure . . . and maybe the problem is I'm afraid to give up the forty-nine percent. Maybe it's 'cause I know the answer implies a sacrifice, that I'm stalling and philosophizing instead of living it out. Getting closer to the horizon also means leaving where you came from—and I don't know if I want to leave from this spot."

"There's that Gide quote," The Beast recalled. "'One does not discover new lands without consenting to lose sight of the shore for a very long time.'"

"Yeah," Slim replied. "Reminds me of Eliot: 'We shall not cease from exploring and at the end of our exploration we will return to where we started and know the place for the first time.'"

"Yeah . . . but we aren't leaving as much as going toward something else. I always promised myself I'd never be one of those people who said 'those four years in college were the best years of my life.' I think it comes down to searching for those moments that make us feel alive. Not to get stuck with monotony like robots. We're programmed to want to evolve. It's hard to get up some days, but you still do it, right? Way too early in my opinion. Up and at 'em by sunrise . . ."

"Ever since the award ceremony I've been waking up mad early," Slim replied.

"Yeah . . . and you banging pots and pans to make an omelet means I'm up, too," The Beast laughed. "You can talk about *carpe diem* as much as you want—mornings are hell. I won't stand for them. I've never done anything worthwhile before ten a.m. Maybe when I'm older I'll start to appreciate them, but as for now, mornings are death."

"Good luck with that next year," Slim said. "You'll have morning workouts. Sleep is sacrificed."

"Sleep is the only thing I absolutely refuse to sacrifice. Unless it's for the best pick at the market. The only thing worse than waking up during a dream is getting woken up by a screeching alarm. How can you start your day like that? How is that a way to enter waking life? One day there will be some devastating study about a whole population constantly waking up alarmed."

Kind of Blue culminated with "Flamenco Sketches (Alternate Take)." We relished the solemn trumpet.

"You mentioned food, Lockart?" Slim seemed to wake. "How about I put some of *my* music on? I could definitely go for a couple of burgers now that we're stuck in here for a Boys' Night."

14

He'd come in the day before reeking of whiskey. In retrospect I should've told them about Dykes's last visit. It went like this:

"Quinbee's been banned and they've got your IP address. But I finally talked to Coach Brees. Boy, could I use a drink!"

His face was swollen. His receding hairline was wet and grotesque, strands of hair sticking to his skull as if they were painted on. Although three standing fans whirred in the bar, none of them seemed to cool him down. Globules of sweat dripped from the tip of his nose. A few more lingered on his upper lip.

He breathed heavily and drank his Red Label in one swig. "I always knew there was something strange about him . . ."

"Oh yeah?" I said nonchalantly. I neither cared nor wanted to know what Dykes was talking about.

"It was because of the 'Meet the Prospects' interview. Brees finally responded to my emails. Said he'd agree to meet me at Quiznos for a quick drink."

"Quiznos, right." I put on a Bill Evans record.

"But someone's been flagging me on Facebook. Twenty times in the past week! I couldn't have sent more than ten messages to Milo, and he'd never rat on me. I trust him. Another drink?"

I poured Dykes another whiskey. He sat on the bar stool with his back hunched over, his forearms slowly sinking into the bar. I didn't say anything, per usual. I preferred to let him speak. "And Gerald, well, I only sent him one. You know how it is . . . people always trying to bring me down. You don't have an account, do you? I mean, so I can keep up with what they're doing?"

Dykes balled up his turquoise windbreaker and dropped it on the floor. "I try to help them out, you know? Can I have another shot? And is that so wrong? To talk to them? To make them feel liked?" Dykes swigged his third Johnny Walker in five minutes. I told him to take a break. "Doesn't matter anyway. Like I said, we went to Quiznos for a drink. And you know what he said to me? He said he doesn't know why The Beast punched him and that The Beast just went berserk for no reason. They were running sprints or something when Coach Brees said, 'What do I have to do, light a fire under your ass? Turn the gas on, Hugh!' And that's when he got punched."

"A real shame. Understandable, though, given the circumstances," I replied.

"Understandable! He almost killed him; that's the point. And didn't you ever wonder why he only got sentenced to The Skillet? Didn't you think it strange to punish attempted murder with flipping burgers? So did I, and I was right. I always knew there was more to it."

"I never thought about it at all, to be honest."

"I always knew there was something off about it. That's why I wanted to talk to Coach Brees. And once he saw the interview, well, he finally agreed. I've got the papers to prove it."

Dykes tapped on his pocket. "But it's over now; he's done. All that research finally paid off. Persistence is everything. Anyway, what a day! Let's celebrate. How about another whiskey? You know it couldn't have been Sam's parents, they're too old to use the Internet." He went off on a monologue, rattling off names that could have reported him. "Toby—that's got to be it. Toby. His parents must've hacked into his account or something. No privacy these days, the bastards. Jesus Toby," he spoke softly. "If I've told you once, I've told you a thousand times: you've got to change your password every two weeks."

Dykes inhaled his fourth whiskey, which I hoped would shut him up. "Like it's a big deal that I sent twenty messages," he continued. "They weren't that long, anyway. Brief things. The last message doesn't make any sense unless you read the rest. *They take it out of context.* That's what everyone does, right? *Of course* it *sounds* weird unless you know the whole story. But they don't know about the beginning. About how we first met. 'Threatening his innocence' . . . come on! Me? I'm the one preserving it! All I ever did was give him a shoulder to cry on. All I ever did was help. Another whiskey please."

I explained I couldn't serve over four drinks in less than twenty minutes.

"I'll wait then. I've got time. Is that really a rule, Lockart? Anyway, it's not like I invited him to live in the cabin, okay? It's not like I asked him to do anything wrong. I just said over summer break it'd be nice to bond. You know, share some meals together, make him feel at home. His parents might as well be estranged. They ignore him all the time, you know? Have I told you about him? Toby? What a great kid. His dad's some big businessman, travels everywhere. Mom's a drunk. He's great, though, really. He needs me, you know? But one thing gets read out of context and bang—well I don't need to explain it to you Lockart, I'm sure you know how it goes." I didn't, and he was quiet for a moment. "But you don't have an account. Maybe I could open one for you? What do you say? I'd take care of all of it. It could be good for business, you know? You'd get a lot of likes, that's for sure. But like I said, they have your IP address now . . . you might be banned, too. Shit. I don't know how it works, to be honest. It's like no one has any respect for privacy anymore."

Dykes put his right hand on the bar and slowly moved it toward my own, which was resting on the edge of the counter next to my glass of water. His splayed fingers continued to inch toward mine, crossing diagonally. As his pinky finger made a move to caress my wrist, ever so slightly with just the tip, I turned around and poured a drink to make sure he got the message.

"Is that water you're drinking?" he asked. "What are you, a pussy?"

I responded with my back still turned. "Yeah, that's it."

Dykes's voice was over-excited and creepy. "You know it's really nice to talk to you. I like this bar. And this stool. And this whiskey. Just promise me one thing, Lockart. Once it's all over and my nephew comes back, will you still drink with me? Will you still let me come to your bar once it's done?"

I pretended I didn't understand. For a time we didn't speak. Not knowing who or what he was talking about, I didn't feel in the least bit alarmed. But as always, without invitation, Dykes started up again soon enough. " . . . Too much effort, you know? And I hurt my ankle, and my knee started to give out. And obviously with the knee I couldn't do anything . . . you know I couldn't use it for weeks? Nothing you can do about a bum knee. I've always had health problems, though. I'm not one of those people who's had an easy life, but I just don't see any use in crying over broken marbles . . . I mean, it's time he faced the facts. You mind if I take some peanuts for Larry?"

I wasn't interested, but Dykes was pathologically incapable of taking a hint. "Lockart? Hello? Lockart? Are you listening?"

"What is it Chandler? I'm tired, that's all."

"Peanuts. Can I have some? I'm not leaving, I just want some for later, that's all. You know, Larry gets really scared during thunderstorms, and I don't want to leave him, so I make sure I have enough supplies. He's like a dog, you know? Cowers in the corner during the lightning. Anyway, I'll stay with him. He's a cute guy, that's all. I wish you could meet Toby, though. Really I do. It would've been such a nice summer . . . oh well. You know, my nephew used to come out to my cabin back in Stoke Ridge? But he ran away, like I said. He always was a problem child. Arrogant, you know? Too self-interested. Wouldn't ever listen—he just talked and talked and talked."

I stared at the black-and-white clock on the far side of the wall, counting the seconds. I couldn't stand looking at Dykes when he got like this: agitated, fast talking, sweating profusely. I usually tried to come up with a reason to get him out. It was his voice that got to me most, the constant grating, the consistent whine. And I hated that he always spoke in questions. "Do you have any Schweppes, Lockart? I want a whiskey ginger."

"All I've got is Canada Dry."

"But I prefer Schweppes. That's too bad you don't have it."

I didn't respond.

"Well okay," Dykes lamented. "I guess I'll have Canada Dry then."

"Red or black whiskey?"

"I prefer the blue."

I sighed. "We've been through this a thousand times, Chandler. It hasn't changed since the first day I saw you. Red or black. No blue. That's all I've got."

"You know blue's the best though, right? I don't know why you don't get it. Have you heard about Beverly? It sounds like she's a big one. Larry will be scared all right! I've bought boards for the windows and everything . . . want to help me put them up?"

"I've got my own house and bar to work on Chandler . . . maybe another time."

"Oh, okay . . . yeah, another time then. Hurricanes, wow. There's some crazy stuff out there, Lockart. You have to stay informed, right? It's scary out there. Did you hear about that orphan that was mutilated in the Congo? I mean things that'll make your skin crawl. The world is really going to shit, isn't it? I mean, I really think we're screwed."

I put on a louder record to try and encourage some type of silence. The Oscar Peterson Trio calmed me down, but when I turned back around, Dykes had his laptop out. The screen was facing my direction, and Dykes's was hovering above it, grinning, pointing at the screen.

"Look at this one. Yikes!" A drop of sweat plopped onto the keyboard, which he wiped off with his palm. "And right here, not far from town. Picture this, Lockart. An eleven-year-old kid walks into school. When it comes time to trade his crackers, he pulls out an Uzi and blows a kid's arm off! Thankfully—get this, it's crazy!—thankfully, most of the kids had armor plated backpacks on! But then, get this, then he goes back to his locker where he's got a rifle with armor-piercing—"

"CHANDLER!" I cut him off. "I told you I've got no use for it. Get it out of here, NOW. I won't ask again: can you please take the computer off my bar?"

Dykes corralled the computer and stuffed the laptop in his backpack. He hugged it close to his chest. "I just thought you wanted to be informed. No need to get angry, Lockart. You know it's a dangerous world out there. There are some crazy people around. That's why you have got to keep up with it. Stay informed, you know? I mean, thankfully I figured out this wacko basketball player they call The Beast. I want to protect my nephew, that's all. You can never be too sure. Speaking of, do you have an alarm system here? You should think about it, Lockart. People die, you know, all the time. You can be sure I won't be leaving my house tomorrow, what with Beverly coming. A woman got flattened by an airborne truck in the Outer Banks. So better board up the windows and all. I think I'll stay in the bathroom. Probably safest in the bathtub? Do you want to come over, actually? I have some spare room. I could make a run to Harris Teeter, buy some whiskey and snacks. Peanuts for Larry, too. That'll be great, we'll stay together."

"Chandler, I've got a wife."

"Bring her along! We can weather the storm, all of us, before I drive up to Milwaukee."

I turned away and pretended to be occupied with the record player. When I turned back around, at least the computer was gone; but Dykes was still bear-hugging his backpack like a scared schoolboy, twittering on about inconsequential nonsense.

" . . . Unless they come here of course. But even then, I think I'll wait. What is this, elevator music? Don't you have some heavy metal? I need something angrier."

"It's Oscar Peterson. I'm not changing it. I don't do heavy metal."

"Peterson . . . never heard of him. He must make a killing in hotels and malls! Heavy metal though, seriously. It'll get you pumped up. Check it out. Hate Inc. Have you heard that song, 'Kill 'Em All'?"

"I don't listen to that kind of thing."

"Well, Hate Inc. What a band. There's also this song called 'Face Saw.' Oh man. Anyway, like I was saying, my nephew. I showed you the picture, right?"

I didn't ask for Dykes to show me, but of course he did anyway. Once again, there he was: a Polaroid of thirteen-year-old Slim.

"Might as well have been my son. I mean, it's really one in the same. Or is it one and the same? The expression?"

"Brother or sister?"

"What?"

"Your nephew. Is he the son of your brother or sister?"

Dykes became flustered. "It doesn't matter, Lockart. What *matters* is he abandoned me. He left me in the lurch, that's all. And I took care of him from day one, trying to be a good fath—uncle, trying to show him the way because the kid was always just a runt . . . a runt who wouldn't have made anything of himself if it wasn't for me."

Dykes sat down, dug his fists into the bar, and scratched at the hardwood. His fingernails were yellow. Their cuticles were mangled. "He looks like me too, kind of. But do you know what I'm saying? But just . . . well, he didn't understand. He was young and foolish, you know?"

"Yeah. Right."

"Well good. I'll have another drink then. You're always so understanding, Lockart. But and the thing is he went off the deep end. I mean, I never did anything wrong. Just like with Toby, blown out of context. People just don't understand. I mean, sure, I might've been a bit too rough on him at times but that's . . . it's not a good place, you know . . . Stoke Ridge? What with that faggot General Haith running it . . . well not anymore. Did you hear what happened last week in Lejeune? So yeah, you've gotta be tough. Only way to survive in this here world of ours. And I'm not one of these jackasses like The Beast who has everything handed to them. I'm not one of these guys who doesn't know what it means to suffer, who's a big college basketball star and has everything going for him. And now he's thinking about not going to the NBA? He's a disgrace to kids everywhere. He should be put in jail. He's bad for sports. But in the end you can't be a good person if you haven't seen what's wrong with everyone? Like, the more you have to suffer, the better person you become? And trust me, I've seen a lot and I turned out all right. But these idiots like General Haith, with their middle-class lifestyles and their money and their houses, trying to set arbitrary rules because they—they're worthless human beings, that's all. Because they don't know what it's like to experience real pain. They're tourists, that's all. I have to live with it daily. So that makes me strong. You know my back hurts all the time? And my knee gets swollen every day. And my dad just died; I mean that's been hard, too. But I'm a man, I can deal with it. Not like The Beast. Not like those faggots . . ."

A smaller voice entered his throat as he started pacing. The light shone bright on his sweaty cranium. I no longer even attempted to respond. "Faggots. Idiots. God, I hate them all. And they say it's me who's got the problem. Ha. I'm trying to help, and these queers are telling me I'm the problem?"

"Easy Does It" came on, which seemed to make Dykes nervous. I turned the music off quickly. My goal was to get him out of the bar.

"Here Chandler, drink this. Take a deep breath. You're fine."

Dykes took the glass of water without thanking me. "What is this, water? Thank god you turned that off . . . I can't stand that new age jazzy crap. How can you—"

"Oscar Peterson isn't—"

"Oh come on, it's all the same shit, Lockart. Jesus Christ. Grow up."

I cursed myself for responding. By that point it'd become futile. I'd never felt this threatened before; Dykes stared through me with rabid eyes. " . . . It's the only way it can be, to expose him. To get him back. Now that I've got proof, I'll be famous. All hail Chandler Dykes.

Why'd you give me water? I don't drink this shit. I want whiskey. It's been thirty minutes. One last one and them I'm off."

I didn't abide. He returned to pacing back and forth, his footsteps pronounced, as if the bar were now a theater and I the audience. And then, without warning, Dykes's voice morphed into something hollow. His eyes became fixated on an invisible spot on the wall. He walked over to the painting. "Why is this called *Nighthawks?*"

"I think it's because of the—"

"I don't like it. It's boring. What's going on? Did you hear what I said earlier? I've figured him out, Lockart. His secret. He'll be exposed. That way I know he won't follow him to the draft, the stupid faggot. Did he think he could get away with it? The past always comes back to bite you in the balls. I mean, what kind of queer opts out? What kind of faggot stays away for six months? Brees is right . . . he's a selfish, entitled cunt. And he deserves to be punished for that. Years I've waited. Thrown out like garbage. And this motherfucker has no respect for his superiors? For the past? Well, I won't allow it. And now that he's done the interview . . . and they expect Brees to remain calm? All because he's a big fancy basketball player and his life is perfect! No, that's not right. So what do you do with a kid who doesn't listen? Daddy never liked using his words either. That's how you learn to tolerate it—grit your teeth and take the punches. You stand there and watch. *Sit there and watch, Chandler. Next time you can help out.* You deal with it, that's all. That's how you become a man. He doesn't know what it's like. He takes it all for granted. We're going to settle this like men. Give me a last shot, Lockart. Don't be a pussy. Here's to the idiots and the queers and all the pussy faggots! It's just you and me, Lockart. Never listening, never playing. Never so much as a goddamned hug."

I refused to serve the whiskey; Chandler stood up and slammed his right fist into the bar. "Never listening, never playing! Never so much as a goddamned hug!"

There was nothing to do but step further back.

"NEVER LISTENING, NEVER PLAYING. NEVER SO MUCH AS A GODDAMNED HUG!"

Chandler crashed both fists down onto the bar, showering the bowl of peanuts onto the sun-drenched wooden floor.

"Get out, Chandler. Now."

"Is this about the peanuts? I'm sorry. I'll pick them up. Larry will eat them. I was just venting. Acting, really. That's all. I'll make some beans for tomorrow night. Anything else from Harris Teeter? What time should I expect you and the wife?"

I made sure his silhouette entered his cabin before I locked up.

15

Slim removed an iPod from his pocket and asked if I had an auxiliary cable. I said I had no idea what he was talking about but he was welcome to look around.

"There, that cardboard box full of cables behind the bar. Some guys came in here to deliver the new sound system."

"New system? Not bad. Why are you classing it up?" Slim asked.

"Jane suggested it. Did it herself, even. Never skimp on music, that's what she always says. I used to play, you know? Jazz piano. Played in a lot of bars just like this one. Well a bit classier, I'll admit it. But I'm retired now."

"Why no piano in here then?"

"I've got one down at the house."

Slim pulled out a wire from the cardboard box and connected it to the gadget, scrolling through his music.

"You know this one, Lockart?" The lyrics started, *Change? Shit. I guess change is good for any of us.* "Best rap song ever written."

We listened without saying a word until the song was over.

"That's lyricism right there. Best of the modern poets, no doubt," Slim said.

The Beast shook his head. "Notorious is still king, I mean, come on. When it comes to lyrics there's no contest. 'Sky's the Limit'?"

"Are you talking about storytelling lyrics? 'Cause there's a big difference. When 2Pac's being honest? I mean, that song's brotherhood incarnate."

"Right, exactly: *when he's honest.*"

"Notorious isn't honest, either," Slim chuckled. "'Big Booty Hoes' is hilarious, though."

"Is that not honest?" I asked innocently.

"Those are moneymaking lyrics, that's all," Slim said. "They hide what's deeper down . . . these guys are young, too. But that's what makes them so great—you can hear the difference. Plus, if there's one line in an entire song that's worthwhile, then it's worth listening to. There's too much bullshit out there to scoff at a good line nowadays . . . you know as well as I do music's taken a turn for the worst."

"Every generation says that," The Beast replied.

"Yeah but this is different. It's the end of the music gold rush, that's why. It isn't real because the musicians aren't real anymore. Most of the sounds are made on computers, and they're still being sold as an image. But now we're starting to see the futility of it all. That's why I'm saying 2Pac talks about what it means to be human. We can all relate to it, somehow."

"Taking off the mask. Sharing it with others," The Beast said. "That's what's hard. But kids coming from shitty backgrounds, of course they're going to envy beauty and getting rich. What do you expect? It's all fine and good to talk about honesty and humanity with a glass of whiskey in a bar. You're not out there in the street though . . . you're not living the struggle."

"Everyone's living the struggle in one way or another. You know as well as I do struggle doesn't end because you have food. But whatever man, that's not the point. I'm not saying I know what it feels like to be a poor black kid in the ghetto—I'm saying I know what he means when he says 'I Ain't Mad at Ya'. *That's* what's human. *That's* why 2Pac and Biggie are the greatest. No one talks about Nelly anymore. But the guys that transcend—Jay-Z and Gang Starr and Wu-Tang—when you hear those guys, it isn't about being poor or rich or an academic . . ."

"Yeah, but a lot of people just listen to those guys because they're told to, for *image*. Like hipsters who follow certain artists because they think it makes them more connected. The question isn't whether or not Biggie or 2Pac is the best . . . the question is *why you think they're the best*. And that's when you find out who really knows their shit—not because there's an objective answer but because someone has an argument for believing."

"I guess it's true," Slim said, "people hear about what's the best or most important without figuring it out for themselves."

"Exactly," The Beast answered. "It's like a sect. They take other people's word for it and never question it. That way they can convince themselves to believe that so-and-so's the best . . . not because they even know what the best really means or why it's the best *for them*, but because it gives them credibility. It makes them sound intelligent. Taking comfort in how other people define you versus trying to define yourself. There's a strange freedom in it, hiding behind it, because you can be lazy. You can seem intelligent. And that way you don't have to look inside. But Lockart, for example, I'm sure you can tell me who you think is the best?"

"Of course I can: best singer? Ella Fitzgerald. Best band? The Beatles."

"And I bet you have good arguments for why, even if you know it's subjective?"

"Yes indeed."

"See," The Beast said. "That's what so many people don't get: you've got to be able to tell me *why*—again, not because it's objective but because in your opinion they're the best. It's easier to say they're the best because *Pitchfork* or *Rolling Stone* says so . . . but think how red-faced most people would get if you asked them to explain."

"They'd cite facts and statistics," Slim guessed. "They'd hand you a resumé as proof."

"Right. But speaking of the best, throw on some Notorious for us, Slim."

As Slim changed songs, The Beast opened the front door to watch the storm. The sky was dark and the rain was pouring. Seen across the parking lot through gray sheets of rain, a squirrel darted between the trees and settled in a small nook. The wind started to howl. There were no animals left in sight. With Beverly now bearing down on us, there'd be no respite before the eye of the storm.

Slim joined The Beast and me on the front porch. "I threw on *Blue Eyes Meets Bed Stuy*," he said. "A mix with Sinatra, for you, Lockart. That shit's insane," Slim pointed at a large, airborne tree limb. "Reminds me of Fran."

"This one's big. I haven't seen a legitimate hurricane in years," I replied.

The sky's belly rumbled. Dull thuds filled the air. Flashes of lightning pulsated behind clouds. We could hear the sound of a single car whooshing down the empty highway.

"Sounds like the traffic let up," The Beast surmised.

"There's no traffic left," I said. "They told everyone to get off the highway and find somewhere safe. Jane told me on the walkie-talkie. Said this one's no joke. Good thing we got the boards up . . . she's always been the wise one."

BOOM! A jolting thunderclap sent The Beast and me indoors. Slim remained on the porch, focused on the thunder, counting the seconds for the lightning.

"You're right!" Slim yelled from outside. "There's not much time now! Those clouds right above are about to pop out something fierce!" *BOOM!* "Five seconds! Did you count that, Hugh?" *BOOM!* "And that one! Oh boy! It's getting seriously close."

Slim was giddy like a child, not in the least scared, drunkenly excited.

"Let's get back inside Slim . . . aren't you hungry?" The Beast proposed.

Slim came in and I closed the back-room shutters. I made a quick pass in the backyard trying to snatch a few branches and other dangerous projectiles. I moved a woodpile to the shed and removed a couple of horseshoes from the sand box. Leaves and debris were starting to fly by. I was soaked within seconds. What had been heavy but manageable rain was now a deluge. The wind howled like a freight train. Whether it was the alcohol or Hurricane Beverly, we were all speaking louder when we returned to the bar.

" . . . But so how do you talk about it without sounding sexual or romantic?" The Beast asked.

"You've just gotta say it and stop pussyfooting around. Stop trying to be so damn pedantic all the time and just talk about it."

"Well." The Beast sipped a beer (we'd gotten off the whiskey by now). "I guess that's where I first found it: beer and basketball."

"Same for me with beer, for a time. That and manning the front lines . . ."

"But that's the problem, isn't it? That we couldn't see it then? And at the end of the day that's what it is: guys sitting together, drinking. All of these acceptable ways to unmask what's engrained—"

"Yeah, but it doesn't last long." Slim sipped his beer. "I came back from Iraq disillusioned as could be. You know, the only time I ever felt an inkling was down at the creek? Of something bigger, I mean. That and talking to you."

"Well, yeah, and Iraq was an escape. You were looking for something, you admit it. But you're right, it's hard to admit loving something, truly, without forcing the issue. I mean, coaches always tried to get me excited before the games, so even with my teammates it was like some illicit relationship. The camaraderie wasn't there. It wasn't like in the movies."

"Same for me with weed," Slim said. "Never made me feel more connected. Granted, it's thanks to the munchies that I first went down to The Skillet. But yeah, maybe I wanted to give up all of that shit. Who knows. I'm certainly glad I did it, spending that summer out in the heat. Maybe I was sick of trying to buy that feeling . . . trying to experience something meaningful like it was something I could eat."

"You can't consume it, that's for sure. Then again, it was the burger that brought us together. I mean, I could tell you weren't just there to get an autograph or talk about basketball. No one had ever cursed at me before, telling me how to cook. It was like you didn't even know who I was—"

"Well I didn't, really. I mean, of course I knew who you were, Hugh, but I didn't give a shit. Why would I want some teenager's autograph? I was high. I wanted a burger. What do I care who's serving me? But you're right. It was a relief. Just a bit of honest conversation. You know, that's the first time in a long time I felt comfortable just speaking. Sure as hell didn't find it in the military. At Stoke Ridge you had to qualify it."

"In the sports world, too . . . *for the love of the game.*"

"Boys will be boys."

"Bros before hoes."

"Boys' night out."

"Brothers in arms," The Beast concluded. "The boys are back in town. But to have a feeling is different than to know how to define it. You know my dad once said that to love a man is to be a man. I didn't know what it meant at the time. Didn't know what to think. But he was right . . . I mean, why do we curb it in secret handshakes and whiskey? Or in punching each other in the arm and smoking weed? Why can't we say why it's so important for us to have other men around? That there's something sacred about watching the game or grabbing a pint?"

"Speaking of burgers, let's transition. I'm hungry!" Slim ended the conversation.

The Beast seemed disappointed, somehow defeated. But he smiled nonetheless. "Well, let's see what we have for fixings."

"I've got a couple pounds of ground beef," I said. "Will that do?"

"Frozen or refrigerated?"

"Who do I look like, Slim?"

"Well, I don't know, Lockart. Sometimes frozen can be alright."

"If it's vacuum-sealed Omaha steaks," The Beast cut in.

"You'll be able to afford those next year in the NBA!" Slim replied. "Now as Hugh knows, and perhaps you do too, Lockart, well, when it comes to burgers, I'm pretty precise about my system. Just like rolling joints and my whiskey, I like 'em how I like 'em, so first thing's first: do you have any—"

"Texas Pete," The Beast finished Slim's sentence.

"I'm not finished yet!" And he proceeded to go through the list: lettuce, sliced tomatoes (not like the Mexicans dice 'em), coleslaw, American cheese, avocado, egg, ketchup, hot sauce. "Like Hugh said, Texas Pete, to be precise."

I went back to the kitchen and confirmed the single avocado. Lightning flashed next door as thunder jolted the bar.

"You got potatoes?" Slim asked.

"Just bought some," I replied.

"We'll bake them in the oven." The Beast was excited. "Garlic and rosemary if you've got 'em. Drizzle some olive oil on top . . . maybe grill up a couple onions?"

"You boys don't mess around," I chuckled as I poured three glasses of water. "Now you two better drink up. Gotta hydrate again. I know you've already had a couple, but rules of the bar. Chug it down nice and fast, just like that. I'll pour you another."

"Wise man, Lockart." The Beast chugged. "Slim, drink up. You keep drinking beer like that and you won't have enough room for dinner. Delayed gratification, you know how it works. And with a good whiskey like Redbreast, there's no pleasure in drinking fast."

Slim chugged his water and refilled his glass. "Worst comes to worst, I'll just be pissing all night . . ."

"Ah, that reminds me." The Beast reached into his pocket and pulled out a ziplock bag filled with green and yellow pills. "Vitamins."

"What is it?" I asked. It was green with yellow dots and smelled like vomit.

"Helps with the hangover," The Beast said. "Trust me. Wellness Formula, it's called."

Slim rolled his eyes. "Yeah, right . . . wellness formula my ass."

The Beast chuckled. "He says it and still ends up taking it every time." The Beast and I took the vitamins with a sip of water.

"Bullshit herbs and vitamin supplements," Slim said. "Placebo effect for people who need convincing."

"Faith in the system, right?"

"Maybe I'm just being polite . . ." Slim replied.

Slim unplugged his iPod and asked me to put on a tune. "Autumn Leaves" by Cannonball Adderley filled the bar.

"Hugh, you want some weed? A little pregame spliff?" Slim pulled out a joint as if he'd been waiting for this moment. "Boys' Night indeed," he said. "Just a couple hits." Slim lit up and closed his eyes. As the tip of the joint turned orange, the trumpet entered the fray.

"You interested, Lockart?" Slim outstretched his hand. I hadn't smoked in years, but I decided to indulge.

"I didn't think you'd be rolling with tobacco . . ." I said. "I thought kids smoked it straight these days."

"Yeah, it's dumb," The Beast laughed as he exhaled the first puff. "Remember when we got high after studying all day on Adderall? And you telling me I was fine and not to freak out?"

Slim laughed. "You were blazed out of your mind—probably gave you too big of a hit."

"I've never been so terrified in my life," The Beast chuckled. "That was the first day I ever did Adderall, too. I'd never felt my brain move so fast. Two hundred pages in three hours. But it got trippy after a while, started to mess with me. I hadn't smoked since the season started, and Slim made me take a full bottle hit! Man, I swear to God, I thought I was going to be *that guy*, you know? Destined for the NBA and then boom. Did drugs, life ruined. Like Len Bias or something, but with weed. I freaked out. Classic bad trip. Remember me sitting on that chair? I couldn't move at all, but I remember you said, 'Dude, no problem . . . I've got this. You sit down. I'll make some tea. You took a big hit. Take it easy. You're fine.'"

Slim smiled. "He was high as a kite, Lockart. Didn't realize it was okay to be that gone."

"Oh, I was freaking out! And then I got even more paranoid and thought you'd think I was a pussy and that I was paranoid or something, and then you'd start thinking something was actually wrong with me, that I was *actually* gone. But then I realized you weren't judging me at all, and you made me a cup of tea. And said you'd been in that situation before. I realized it was okay to be out of control. That's the first time I felt really *safe* getting high."

We smoked the spliff and didn't feel the need to converse. For a time the saxophone took us out of the bar and up past the clouds through sheets of gray rain; and the clarinet took us higher towards some kind of bliss, where the eye of the storm churned; and then the song began to sing a sadder tune once again, sitting on the lower notes until the piano brought us down, where we sat in silence with a nostalgia none of us could place; and once the melody returned we came back to the beginning, and without saying it I realized they'd been searching for *this* all along.

"Man," The Beast said. "That's the best version I've ever heard of that song."

"I'm glad you liked it," I smiled. "What with Miles Davis on the trumpet, Art Blakey on the drums, Sam Jones on the bass, and Hank Jones on the keys? Can't go wrong."

"The weed doesn't hurt either!" Slim laughed. "Sorry to keep changing the music, Lockart, but before we get cooking, do you mind if I put something on? We kind of have a tradition to start off Boys' Night.

Are there speakers in the kitchen? I mean, can we hear it from there? Perfect. Well then, I'll throw on some El Michels before we start."

We went through the hallway and took a right into the kitchen. Slim ducked down. Hugh entered sideways.

"Have you heard of this, Lockart?" Slim asked. "El Michels Affair? Listen to that hi-hat! I can't get enough of it. This Isaac Hayes tribute can keep us going the rest of the night!"

I had already laid out some ingredients on the kitchen island—two tomatoes, a few onions, and the burger buns. I pulled out the rest from the fridge, and Hugh unwrapped the burger meat and tossed it into a metallic mixing bowl. Slim knew his way around the kitchen without even asking: he was already sprinkling powdered garlic, curry, and a pinch of cumin into the meat. He added a dash of olive oil and a bit of balsamic. "We'll wait a second to let it marinate," he said. "Speaking of, Hugh, how was that girl the other night?" Slim picked up the avocado and pinched its sides.

"Ha. Are you talking about Jessica?"

"Whoever it was, the one with the onion butt . . ."

The Beast laughed. "Onion butt? What are you talking about? If you're talking about Jessica, yeah, it was good. Wasn't the first time we hooked up, though. I was seeing her right around Christmas, remember? The first couple times we had sex it was a bit awkward, to be honest . . ."

The horn section was picking up. The Beast was standing at the cooking island, kneading the beef like bread dough, coating his hands with meat fat. Slim stood next to him, tossing the avocado between his hands, rocking side to side.

"I can believe it," Slim said. "Never is that great the first time, anyway. Making love's like breaking in a new pair of shoes."

"Well, sometimes it can be," The Beast responded. "The first time, anyway. She'd just broken up with her boyfriend, so she wasn't really *there* mentally, you know? And I did most of the work. But just recently, the other night, well, I could tell she was at ease. I like her . . . it's too bad we're leaving North Carolina. Anyway, being comfortable is the only way to have great sex——"

"But that takes time, for all parties involved." I listened to Slim. "As if I'm supposed to enjoy it immediately 'cause I'm hard . . . that's wacko, man. I need to be seduced."

Slim went to the fridge and returned with an egg. He cracked it with one hand into the metallic mixing bowl. The Beast continued to knead. Slim went over to the sink to pour the yolk from one shell to another, returning with half an eggshell filled with yellow.

"You know how many girls just lay there expecting me to finish?" Slim poured the yolk in. "As if I could just come on command? The trick is, make them come first. I mean, just 'cause they're smoking hot doesn't give them the right to be entitled. As if *I had to finish* 'cause she was just *so* good. No, some girls suck at sex. There, I said it. Blame can't always be put on the man. But what with all the magazines, they think tits and ass is all I need to make it happen . . . well, I need more than some fun-bags to get me off. Like you said, if she doesn't make me feel at ease? Well, if alcohol's involved, it just isn't happening."

As Slim and The Beast discussed, I took the potatoes out of the pantry and put various ingredients on the kitchen island—lettuce, cabbage, a couple more beers, and the condiments. Slim came over, and I handed him a knife, which he used to cut an onion at the tip and the root.

"And you better believe I've faked it," Slim said as he sliced into the wooden countertop. "Expecting me to have an orgasm without making me feel comfortable? Come on! You better believe I'll be shaking and quaking as if I was coming, too. Girls don't have hegemony over fake orgasms . . . like Kramer said, sometimes it's enough already and you just wanna get some sleep. As long as you make sure you take the condom off quickly, hide it in the trash. And if you aren't using a condom, well, then you've got a bigger issue. That or you're in a committed relationship, in which case you should never be afraid of having to come."

Slim walked over to the sink and peeled off the outer skin of a third onion. He returned to the cutting board and sliced the onion in half, cutting it vertically, following the lines, deep enough to sever but not enough to separate. He turned the onion on its side and sliced it horizontally, swiping the onions on the cutting board into the mixing bowl with the knife.

"Yeah, I've faked it too," The Beast said. "Once or twice. But if it's a bad one-night stand, honestly? I'll finish by whacking off."

"You mean during or afterwards?" Slim asked.

"I mean before we fall asleep. I mean, come on . . . if it's really bad, at least one of the two of us should be able to come."

Once the onions were minced and the avocados sliced, Slim handed me a bottle of Stella he'd opened with his lighter. He splashed some beer into the mixing bowl where The Beast was emptying a pack of bacon bits and sprinkling a bit more rosemary and curry. "And you wonder why so many dudes have trouble coming . . . expected to finish, no questions asked. Plus, after whiskey and beer? At five in the morning? If I'm being honest, I'd prefer a pizza. That happened once, in the dorms. I was having sex and I could hear a couple guys handing out free slices in the hall. I considered getting up. Honest. 'Cause I knew the one-night-stand girl didn't wanna be there either, and that's what killed me 'cause then I thought: what are we doing here? You can be hard and not feel it. She can be wet and want to go home. There was no connection between us, but I didn't go get the pizza. It was like prodding at something that doesn't want to respond. Fucking strangers? I don't know. Not that it can't be great, but the only good one-night stand," Slim said as he finished tearing up some lettuce, "is when both people aren't thinking of anything else. In the moment, plain and simple. There to have an experience."

I cut the tomatoes—circular, not diced—and chopped a few potatoes into cubes.

"Bottom line," Slim said. "When it comes to having sex with strangers, it isn't usually about the girl at all. It's about your dick or ego or pride."

"Or loneliness," The Beast added.

"Yeah, that's what makes me feel really awful. Women deserve better. That's why I always end up feeling like shit. Because if you don't call her again, what do you think she'll start thinking? There's nothing worse than making another human being feel self-conscious. And women have to deal with so much bullshit already . . . I don't want to be one of those guys that's just adding to the pot. And that's on us; it's our responsibility to appreciate women. And maybe part of that means not banging immediately or at least not making them feel like an object, even if it is just for one night."

"I think you said it best—we're talking about human beings," The Beast said. "And whether it's a man or a woman, all of us are terrified of feeling self-conscious. All this talk about guys versus girls . . . maybe we should be talking about humans, plain and simple."

"I totally agree. No inhibitions," I added.

"Of course, there are some things you won't do on the first night," Slim explained, "but you've got to be comfortable enough to have sex the right way. And yes, there is a right way . . . or at least there's a wrong way. I want to make her come with my tongue, my fingers, however I can. And I want her to make me go wild, too."

I went to the refrigerator and pulled out a stack of American cheese. It was the industrial kind wrapped in cheap plastic. I removed the film carefully, making sure not to rip it.

" . . . Jessica came twice," The Beast was saying. "I was seriously proud."

Slim stirred the potatoes in a pot of boiling water. "Are you sure she wasn't faking?"

"Based on my head between her legs and feeling the contractions, I'd say no. But it's possible, I guess . . ."

"Yeah, sounds legit, especially if it wasn't the first time."

"Well, you know me, Slim." The Beast was shaving carrots above the trashcan. "I rarely have 'just one time.' I'm going to miss her a lot, actually. I always preferred something real to having sex for the notches."

"Unless she's so damn sexy you can't do anything but gawk," Slim replied. "That girl in the nurse's outfit? I had no chance."

"Ha. Yeah right."

"You better believe it, man."

"What do you mean, nurse's outfit?"

"I haven't told you this?" Slim smiled. "Well shit! Lockart, bring those over, we'll put 'em in the pan."

I drained the boiled potatoes into a colander before shaking them out onto a baking sheet. The Beast drizzled olive oil on top while Slim sprinkled rosemary and garlic. As I sliced squares of butter for the burger buns, Slim described his exploits while sautéing two onions in a pan:

"I'd hooked up with her a couple times. The first was a one-night stand, actually . . . nothing to write home about. But we kept talking and actually made a real connection, right? All it took was a long dinner. So one night we were drinking and talking and we went back to her apartment to 'watch a movie.' Ha. Isn't that the sweetest sentence you ever heard? A grown woman asking you to come back to 'watch a movie'—I get excited just thinking about it. So there we were in her bed all comfortable with the pillows propped up. By the time the opening credits were finished, both of our clothes were off. And then, I don't know how it came up, but she said she had this nurse's outfit in her closet. It was from last Halloween or something. As soon as she said it, well, I stopped kissing her neck and suspended the whole operation. At first she was all shy about it and said she didn't want to put it on 'cause it made her look slutty and whatnot . . . I told her she was too beautiful not to wear it. But really, there's no way a girl lying on top of you—who's naked, moreover—who mentions a nurse's outfit is going to be embarrassed about wearing it. She was testing her comfort level, maybe. Anyway, I insisted and she abided, and hot damn was she a sight to behold. Beautiful really, like out of a Disney movie or something, almost too perfect, like a cartoon. And at that moment—I swear—she was the sexiest woman alive. And when I told her that? She came over and climbed straight on. And man I'm telling you . . ."

"Climbed straight on . . . you mean—" The Beast surmised.

"Yeah, no condom. I wasn't proud of it, but shit. When the most beautiful woman you've ever seen puts on a nurse's outfit and decides to climb on without a second of hesitation? What was I gonna do, tell her to get off? Man, come on. We all have our limits. Now it's true, she could've been a crazy woman that wanted to have kids . . . but who thinks of reality during great sex?"

Once the onions were dark brown, Slim turned the stove off. "That's gonna be nice. I'll throw 'em in the baking pan to cook with the potatoes. Lockart, throw some butter on it too. Hugh, some more garlic and rosemary on top? We'll leave that to cook, right?"

"Did you turn off the stove?" The Beast asked.

"Yeah I did."

"Check again. So the sex was great?"

"The sex was fine, but her willingness to wear the nurse's outfit was what really made the night."

"I told you about that girl in Berlin, right? The one that picked *me* up at the bar?"

"Hell no you didn't! How'd you forget about that?"

"Well you forgot about the nurse . . ."

"That's 'cause you never asked. So Berlin, let's hear it."

The Beast filled a mixing bowl with mayonnaise, white vinegar, Calvados, and Texas Pete. The cabbage and the onions rounded it out. Slim added black pepper and sea salt as The Beast churned up the coleslaw with a round wooden spoon. "We took a trip a couple of years ago . . . summer league thing for about a week. She was incredible. She had these gorgeous breasts. And her face was sexy, incredibly kind. But to be honest, it was her smile—I know that sounds stupid, but I saw her from the end of the bar and, well, that was it. She was confident, too. She came up to me first. More or less asked me to make out. She took me outside like the ship was going down. Pushed me up against the bus—it was a bar in an abandoned school bus in the middle of a field in Berlin. Go figure. So fast forward to her apartment, well, let's just say she knew how to move around. Laundry machine, kitchen countertop, sofa, shower. You name it—"

"German girl! That's wild . . . can't say I've experienced that."

"But that's not even the craziest part. It wasn't just that she was German, and I mean full-on with the accent, but her dad was from Martinique."

"And she had a German accent?"

"I know! It was exotic in a strange Teutonic kind of way. You just don't expect to hookup with a sexy black girl in Germany. Is that racist? Anyway, as soon I saw her, I knew it was done. I don't even remember her name, to be honest. But the smile I do, and it was amazing sex. Funny in the morning, too: I ended up in an East Berlin tenement with a killer hangover and this gorgeous girl on my arm and no idea how to get back to the team hotel. I took the circle line metro until I found a familiar stop. Never saw her again, but that'll be a memory for life. Something I'll tell my grandkids . . ."

Slim chuckled. "Make sure they're not sitting in your lap . . ."

The Beast added a finely chopped Granny Smith apple to the cole-slaw. "That should do it for the slaw. Family secret recipe . . . Jessica loved it actually. I should call her before we get out of the state—"

"You really have something for her, don't you?" Slim asked.

"It's starting, I think. She gets me, you know? When we're together, it's like time has stopped, and at the same time it's moving insanely fast."

"Sounds like love," I said.

"Yeah, could be. She's just so understanding. Like, the other night we were having sex, but I was all in my head about the draft and some other stuff, and she was cool enough to realize I wasn't going to finish. And she was totally fine with it. Absolutely no stress. After she came she lay down next to me and was fine with caressing my chest. She said she understood, no problem. And of course, because she didn't care if I finished, I ended up coming anyway. And here's the kicker: she made me breakfast in the morning. I mean, that's just generous. That's the key to a good relationship, I think."

"Well, you'll give her a call tomorrow, once we're out of the state. The only girl I ever thought I loved now lives in Paris," Slim said. "It was great between us, for a while. But her departure was always on our mind. Maybe that's what made it so great—knowing it had to end. I should see what she's up to. Maybe I'll take a trip to France someday."

The Beast liked Slim's suggestion. "We should do a trip together . . . I've always wanted to see where my parents cooked. Go to Rungis."

The Beast grabbed a wad of meat from the metallic mixing bowl and formed it into a burger before placing it on wax paper. "So why was she so great? I assume it was more than sex?"

"Well, actually no, not really. It was exactly that. But I'm talking the best sex you can possibly imagine. She let me lick everywhere—and I mean everywhere. Something about that turns me on like crazy."

"I can't say I've ever licked an asshole . . ."

"You're missing out, Hugh. Haven't you ever wondered? And let me tell you, it feels amazing, too. Psychoanalyze me if you want, but she knew how to please. There was no taboo. I wasn't embarrassed. A great relationship without great sex? You might as well just be best friends. She was generous and I was generous. Smart too. A great relationship."

Slim removed six burger buns from a plastic bag and laid them on an oven tray. I placed the butter on the bread.

"Don't put too much on, Lockart. Yeah, that should be enough," The Beast said. "Splash some water on them too . . . helps to keep them from drying out. You know, it's funny that you mention great sex. I don't know how most guys end up getting girls at all. Most guys are idiots when it comes to pleasing women. Why? Maybe 'cause they're selfish, but also 'cause they're not honest with themselves. It's the same dudes that are overconfident in the bar that are also lacking in the bedroom . . . I mean, first and foremost you've gotta respect the woman, and saying you want to fuck her before you even know her name? That's for construction workers, and they're not serious about catcalls—the truth is they'd be terrified if a woman ever stopped. But if you love a woman's body—or a man's, whatever you're into—then you respect it; and respect means not thinking of it like some kind of object. So yeah, you better lick it and make sure she gets off, too. What kind of guy is afraid to go down on a girl? We can whack off and have an orgasm in five minutes, but that's not the point. Enjoying the experience versus focusing on the orgasm—that's where the real pleasure is. Not that they don't compliment each other: the longer you last, the better you come, right? You can throw on the cheese now, Lockart. The potatoes are about done."

I placed six cheese slices on the hamburger buns. "Hold up, don't put 'em in just yet, Lockart," Slim said. "I'm not trying to have cheese dripping down on my hands. You know I got a second-degree burn from a goddamned Hot Pocket? Look at my hand, see that mark on the edge? But Hugh, you've gotta love your body first. And that's the key, right? Self-confidence. And men have a huge problem with self-image, they just don't talk about it. And what with these fucking magazines and TV shows and Botox and what not? Well, it's easy to look in the mirror and squeeze your belly fat. I mean, easy for us to say, we're both jacked as shit, no doubt . . . but we've also put in the hours. But some people hate themselves . . . literally can't stand to look in the mirror, shaving in the shower, brushing their teeth in the kitchen. I did it for a time, couldn't stand to look at my scar. And then, it's a shame to say it, but some people just aren't attractive. Shit, look at Sgt. Dykes! But there's nothing you can do about it, you have to live with it. And I imagine it's no walk in the park for someone like that—"

"Right, but that's the beauty of sex, isn't it?" The Beast said. "That in the moment you forget. You're with the person, not the body. Or is it possible to forget about the body during sex? Whatever the case, self-confidence is essential. So you have to make her feel sexy. And she has to make you feel sexy, too."

"Yeah," Slim said. "But if you tell her she's the most beautiful thing you've ever seen, you better believe it. Women are perceptive; they know when you're saying it just to get in the sack. That's why so many guys' game is so shitty, unless she just wants to use *them* for sex. But then when she doesn't call back, they call her a slut . . ."

Slim used his thumb to create a slight indentation in the six raw burgers sitting on the wax paper. "See, that's the main problem: making girls feel self-conscious. Cowardly move. How many times have you had sex with the lights on? It doesn't make any sense . . ."

"Most girls assume they're unattractive 'cause society tells them to be hotter," The Beast surmised. "And then they get all competitive and fashion-y about it and end up being part of the problem . . ."

"Girls like attention, but they like the prospect of attention more," Slim opined. "The longer you wait to talk to her the better . . . unless you want to stand in line just to flirt like most of the other guys in the bar. But those are the types whose go-to insult is saying you've got a small dick, which is hilarious. Then, of course, you've got the girls who attribute importance to the size of your cock, too. On the darker side you've got the insecure girl who's been taught that women are supposed to be submissive, and on the other hand you've got the princess type who expects expensive shit all the time 'cause somehow being a woman means getting presents. Those are extremes, sure, but that's reality, too. And unfortunately those types represent a decent portion of society. Keep it human, that's what I say—forget about man and woman for a second, that's all. All of us get lonely. All of us want to be hugged. The second you start talking about gender norms and tradition and how it's the man who's supposed to do this or that or vice versa . . . well that's when things start fragmenting and get confused, which is why you've got jackasses throwing out one-liners at the bar and their female counterparts who get turned on by loud motorcycles and red cars."

"But that's the extreme," The Beast said. "And it's getting better, I think. Women are better off now than they were in the twenties, no doubt. But that doesn't mean we can't hold the door or buy dinner or flowers. I've always secretly wanted to throw my jacket on top of a puddle—"

"Nice idea in principle, but I'm not ruining my jacket so a girl's shoe won't get wet," Slim replied.

"No, but you get the point. Women deserve to be treated well," The Beast concluded.

"So do men," Slim said. "Respect and generosity. Those are the keys. We're all human."

16

As the potatoes cooked and the buns simmered, we passed through the screened-in back porch to check up on Beverly. The wind would've blown a lesser man clean off his feet. The rain hit us horizontally, stinging us in the face. The Beast stayed at the threshold 'cause he didn't want to get wet; either that or he was afraid to step outside. There was a darkness overhead like I hadn't seen in years. Leaves and debris cast darting shadows across the landscape. The wind howled and hissed. Thankfully, I'd brought the wind chimes inside. The rain engulfed the violently swaying trees. Beverly had sucked up all but a pale light in the sky. Lightning struck again and again, shattering more than a few trees behind the bar. Black clouds pelted the swampy backyard with penny-sized raindrops, engorging deep puddles and forming torrential streams. And then a bolt of lightning seemed to rip the sky in two. The bar's foundations shook with a thunderous *BOOM*. Without hesitation, we all scrambled back inside. Slim said the thunder reminded him of artillery fire. The Beast was already back in the kitchen, his voice competing with the deafening rain on the roof: "Jane just called on the walkie-talkie! Said a tree fell in the yard. She's going down to the basement to be safe. Category five, they're saying! Bigger than Hurricane Hugo, even!"

I called Jane back to make sure she was all right. Although I was happy to be with Slim and The Beast, I wished she'd been by my side that night.

"We're in for a ride!" Slim said gleefully, holding onto the kitchen island like he was below deck in a squall. "Is this bar high up enough to be safe from flooding?"

"Far enough away from New Hope Creek, sure," I replied. "But I'm worried about my house. Not for the water . . . but there are trees all around."

"I'm sure she'll be alright! Creek or no creek . . . I'm talking about the rain, Lockart! Did you see your backyard?" Slim said. "Looks like you're going to have a new pond."

"It's got a thirty-five-mile eye," The Beast remarked, wiping his face with a dish towel. "You see the way the trees are bending? Jane said if we hear another thunder crack like that to stay low to the ground. What about Dykes's cabin? He's going to get smashed."

"He's doesn't have a basement," I said. "But he'll be alright."

We huddled around the kitchen island. "Who the hell's worried about Dykes?" Slim said. "During Hurricane Fran, two trees fell right next to my house. I remember my mom didn't even budge, high as a goddamn kite. There was a weeklong state of emergency in Chapel Hill for that storm, and that was a Category 3. Category 5, you said? Remember Floyd in '99? That was a Category 4. The creek came up to the edge of my trailer. Afterwards, I remember seeing dozens of dead and dying crawdads. You know they retired Floyd's name?

Hurricane Hall of Fame. Good thing we boarded up those windows, Lockart. Jane's a keeper, no doubt!"

As Slim said this, a tree branch slammed into the bar.

"I want to see it, just real quick." The Beast made a decision. "I loved watching hurricanes as a kid. Just a quick step outside."

"Hugh, not a good idea. You heard what Jane said. Tell him, Lockart."

"I'm literally taking one step out. Just to see what it's like. Come with me. Why not?"

Despite my protests, Slim and The Beast stepped into the breach. The rain challenged The Beast's footing as he made his way outside. Slim stayed behind, calling out flying debris. The Beast crouched down low, struggling against the wind like a stumbling weather reporter. A gust blew a tree branch across the backyard. It hovered in the air for just a moment before slamming into my summer grill, not five feet away from where The Beast was crouching. Pinecones and pine needles battered his body as he trotted back. He was soaking wet, complete with a giddy smile. "Holy shit, did you see that! That branch almost smashed me in the face! Man, what a rush. That wind is seriously strong. I don't know how those trees are staying up. You sure we're safe, Lockart? Slim, you want to have a go? That's enough for me . . . let's throw the burgers on the pan. I'll get it hot."

"Let's finish our beers, first," Slim replied. "Stay on the back porch for a second. We'll stay here, behind the screen door. It'll keep us safe, right?"

"Not likely," I said doubtfully. "I wouldn't stay out here too long. Just before the eye hits . . . that's when it's the worst. I'm going to call Jane. If you boys are gonna stay here, be wise."

As soon as I said it, a massive pinecone ripped through the screen door. I heard The Beast speak a few words to Slim as I walked back to the kitchen: " . . . smoke another spliff. Front row seats, just for a second. I'm glad to be here with you, Slim. These are the times."

As Slim and The Beast sat in rocking chairs on the back porch, creaking back and forth as they puffed on the joint, watching the curtain of water approach with the storm, and speaking over the symphonic *BOOMS*, the heavy wind, and the deafening rain, I was glad they were together and that I was on the walkie-talkie with Jane. Brilliant flashes illuminated the bar. Thunder cracks shook even the bravest of dogs. And although pine trees surrounded us and the back-yard water was rising, I wasn't afraid for the time being; I knew Jane was safe and someone was watching the bar. Slim and The Beast weren't afraid either so long as they were together. There are few sounds more serene than the torrent of heavy rain.

After returning from the upstairs bedroom 'cause I couldn't get good reception in the kitchen, I told Slim and The Beast that I'd be joining Jane during the eye.

" . . . Yeah but it doesn't make the essential difference," The Beast was saying as I joined them in the kitchen.

"Essential difference, of course not," Slim responded. "Too much and you just become an idiot. And it's true, there does come a time when they just aren't productive anymore. Instead of illuminating the feeling, it masks what you're looking for. Like when you smoke before chess or *NBA 2K* or insist on getting high for a late-night conversation. It's there all along, but weed masks it sometimes. It can take you *away* from making that connection . . ."

"But it can also improve it," The Beast responded.

"The bottom line is moderation, I think. It's not like we *need* it to enjoy these times. But it's not like because we just smoked a couple of joints we're in the wrong, either. We didn't always smoke when we played video games, right? Or just sitting in silence together, doing our homework and whatnot. We only smoked on weekends. But that right there's the essential difference, isn't it? Knowing when to stop. That and talking about it—I mean, that's what this is about, being honest. 'Cause all those moments I'm talking about, both of us were truly *there* and listening to each other. Before we started hanging out, it wasn't so easy to make that connection. When I was getting high all the time, I was forcing the issue. And that's probably 'cause I thought it *was* essential to create an experience. But I also smoked to avoid the situation, to get out."

The Beast took a moment to respond and seemed somewhat serious. "Escaping. I think about it all the time." He stopped cooking the burgers for a moment before shaking his head and returning to the task. "But no. It's not escaping. It's seeing something else. I don't think getting drunk or getting high is simply escapism . . . I'm not saying it's some hippy bullshit about *what IS reality?* But I'm more honest when I'm drunk and more perceptive when I'm high. And I feel most connected when I'm drinking with you, Slim, so saying it's simply escapism is too easy in my mind . . ."

"Can you pass me that pan, Lockart?" Slim asked. "It's about time for the fried eggs. I think you're right, too."

I handed Slim a frying pan. He drizzled in the olive oil and turned on the heat. "Okay, so we're high now. What are we trying to escape?"

The Beast stared intently at the frying pan, studying the olive oil as it dispersed.

"Or are we seeking experience?" Slim continued. "Maybe those are one and the same . . . I mean, what's scary about a bad high is exactly that, right? That you've escaped reality for a different experience, an experience you no longer want to be in. Like a stranger in your own novel—"

"That's it!" The Beast exclaimed. "*A stranger in your own novel.* Even now, just a second ago, I had a second of thinking, 'Fuck, I'm too high. I'm going to ruin Boys' Night because I got too high and I'm going to have to manage someone that isn't exactly me all night.' But thankfully, I've realized it's okay to be high and to just go with it. You taught me that. The best way to get over it is to talk about it, right? But having the balls to voice that fear is something totally different. You started smoking early though? Like what, thirteen?"

"Way too early for my own good." Slim shook his head. "I can tell you that much. On second thought, I'll fry these at the last minute so they're piping hot, all right? I'd been smoking for years on account of the secondhand from my mom . . . but it's 'cause I didn't have friends that I did it in the beginning. Or maybe I was afraid I couldn't make 'em. Either way, I smoked to try and fit in. I wanted people to invite me to their birthday parties, so I started selling weed. I was damn-near rich, but not like I wanted to be. I never biked around a neighborhood or played hide-and-seek. I never got pizza or played late-night board games or flashlight tag. The only way I could make friends was with weed, and they were usually older kids who didn't really care about me. Just got me in trouble."

"And your mom didn't give a shit?"

"Wilhelmina encouraged it! Or at least she would have if she'd known I was dealing. She was too high to care, really, always outside mowing the lawn. But no, she never said anything when someone came over to pick up, so that's how I made friends in the beginning. Didn't last long though . . . soon I got sent off to Stoke Ridge."

"Sent? Didn't you want to go?" I asked.

"Well yeah, in principle at least. Apparently I didn't have the papers, but Dykes begged Stoke Ridge to let me in. General Haith didn't want to let me in at first . . ."

"But you liked General Haith . . ."

"I grew to love him. But I think he always knew I didn't really belong. He was a career soldier, by the books. All about respect. And he didn't trust Dykes. He resented that Dykes paid his way into the academy, too. So anyway, Haith figured Dykes had some weird sexual thing for me . . . tried to fire Dykes multiple times. But in the beginning I admired Dykes. Plus, I was glad to get out of public school. I didn't deal much at the academy, but after Iraq I picked it back up. All the cocaine being sent to me, too. People trying to frame me. I made a killing off of it. Anyway, I stopped dealing once I met you. The last street sale I ever did was that day at The Skillet!"

"So you stopped immediately?" I asked.

"Well, pretty quickly. No longer felt the need to get high. Plus, I had more money than I knew what to do with. Frat kids spend their allowance on coke and weed and whiskey, thinking they've earned it 'cause they went to class or some shit. Anyway, you were actually interested in talking, Hugh. And I knew you weren't interested in drugs . . . plus you had no idea about all the rumors circulating about me." Slim sipped his beer and let it linger in his mouth before continuing. "But it wasn't just talking . . . we could also sit together in silence, right? See, I used to talk people around in circles lest they see through me. I figured silence meant weakness. I thought it meant I was uninteresting . . . probably 'cause I was afraid no one was really listening. But the last thing you wanted was more noise, right? You had your own rumors to deal with, so we got along immediately. Not that the silence is gonna last, is it Hugh! This man's gonna be a top-ten pick, Lockart!"

Slim raised his beer. The Beast pretended he didn't hear him. "Hugh! Top-ten pick! Don't leave us hanging on the cheers!" The Beast clinked bottles with us both, but he wasn't convinced. "Yeah. I don't know about that. Maybe it isn't the right decision . . ."

"Oh not this again . . ." Slim shook his head.

"No. Hold on a second. I'm serious, Slim—"

"Well shit, you've already made the decision! We're driving up to Milwaukee, aren't we? There's no going back now. This isn't about Jessica, is it?"

"No, it's not about Jessica. It has nothing to do with—"

"And that's part of being an adult, right? Like you said, tough decisions. Choosing to go down a path that might not lead the right way."

"Right path. There is no right path. The right path is the one you choose. And I know it seems obvious, what with my size and all. Not to mention the money. And I never really thought about it until my parents died . . . until recently I just kind of assumed playing in the NBA was the right thing to do. But then the Jim Brees thing happened and I got away from the game and realized that I can live without it . . . basketball I mean. All those months away from it? I didn't lose any sleep. And even now, sitting here. I don't know if it's the right decision. I'm going to be playing for other people . . . they're going to be making money off of me. And I—"

"You're going to be making a shit load off them, too! What, do you want to make burgers the rest of your life? Sit around drinking, talking to me?"

"Well yeah, maybe. What if I do? But you know that's not what I mean. This isn't about The Skillet. I doubt whether or not I have the passion for the game. And like I've told you, Slim, it's complicated. There are contracts and papers and things to wrap up with UNC . . . it's not just about going to the NBA or not."

"Well, you and I are driving up to Milwaukee, to the NBA Draft no less. And we've talked about this, Hugh: worst-case scenario, you go for a couple years, save up, and get out. Take advantage of the system . . . finally get back at UNC. Why are you still worried about them? You've got a degree. You're finished."

"You know as well as I do it doesn't end with graduation. It's not over just because of the—well, I don't want to get into it. *The point is* maybe I don't want to play in the NBA. I mean, look at me, I'm having doubts before I even get picked! Didn't you ever wonder why I finished most games on the bench?"

"Well yeah, 'cause of the foul trouble. Or getting ejected. You're telling me you preferred being on the bench at the end of the game?"

The Beast didn't say anything. Neither did Slim.

"Fifty-one, forty-nine," The Beast broke the silence.

"What do you mean?"

"That's where I am: Fifty-one percent of me thinks I should go, forty-nine percent thinks—"

"That you should go back to The Skillet?"

"Not The Skillet, Slim! Not Chapel Hill either. I don't know where, that's the problem. But I know where I don't want to be. And maybe it's like you said, the problem of adult decisions. Having to choose between two options that are scary as shit."

"Well Hugh, you know what I think. You're the best goddamn player in the country. You can't pass up that opportunity. You know how much money you could make in a single season? You think you're better than trying?"

"Not better than trying. But maybe I'm past it. I've always done what's expected of me. What others want me to do for their benefit. And I've been okay with it, responding in that way. But I'd be lying if I told you I didn't feel safer on the bench. I always got nervous about finishing games, didn't I? For all the love I had for basketball, when it came down to the last second? I preferred being a spectator. I didn't want to participate."

"Well, next year you're going to have to play late-game. The Bucks are horrible. Jesus. They haven't been—"

"I'm not going to be the number one pick . . ."

"Of course you are! The Bucks haven't been good since Kareem. But with The Beast in town? Come on man . . . it's a new generation."

"But that's exactly what I'm talking about—The Beast is just a nickname. You're the one who calls me Hugh. And the person you know, the guy you met down at The Skillet, that's who I am, really. And that guy isn't sure if he wants to play anymore. The Beast is just a caricature. Maybe he's the one whose jersey is retired at UNC. That's who everyone says I am, but do I agree with it? When I'm honest with myself, no. When no one expects anything from me, I want to be the guy in the kitchen who loves to play basketball but also loves good conversations and good whiskey and a joint."

"Why can't you be both?"

"Because this is one of those decisions. And that's what I'm trying to say—I don't know who I want to be. I don't know what I want to become. All I know is what I'm not."

"But you're a goddamn phenom when it comes to the game. You've got a gift, Hugh. You've got a responsibility to use it."

"Fifty-one percent. And size isn't a gift."

"You just said it was the other way 'round . . ."

"Well, that's the problem, isn't it? Which one is it? The question is: do I have the balls to make a real decision? Because if that's what we're talking about, that's the logical conclusion. I'd be lying if I said this was about something else, anyway. Even as we're driving to Milwaukee . . . do I want to go to the NBA? And neither you nor Coach Brees nor ESPN nor the memory of my parents is going to convince me . . ."

"But if you go you'll make millions!"

"You're right. And I'll keep playing a game. And I'll keep asking myself that question. The best and worst question: what could I have become?"

"Well shit." Slim clasped his hands together. "For the sake of argument, let's say it isn't your thing. What are we talking about then?

You're a seven-foot college basketball legend with a BA in literature who chose *not to go* to the NBA. You might get a documentary out of it. You're already getting one, that's true. Maybe they can end it with you flipping a burger and smiling into the camera as you say some cheesy line. I know, I know, it's not what we're talking about. But what *are* we talking about? You want to be a cook? Fine. But your future isn't The Skillet. You said be honest, well let's say it: this idea you have about cooking is about your parents, isn't it? Go on, you can say it. Okay, so maybe you're doing it for them, fine. Or maybe you're doing it 'cause you're really passionate about cooking after all. But you're idealizing last summer, you're idealizing your parents' life. It's harsh, I know, but you've gotta move on. Sure, you could become a cook, start from the bottom, work your way up. But the real question isn't what do you want out of life as much as what are you willing to sacrifice?"

"That's a good question. But talent is work, it's not a gift. And my body has a shelf life. My knees aren't good. My ankles are shit. Some of the scouts have already noticed it. But it's not about my physiology . . . those are just excuses. The only gift I've ever had is being willing to put in the hours. And maybe I'm afraid of making the easy choice instead of the right one . . ."

"Or maybe you're confusing 'em. Maybe they're one and the same."

"Bullshit. Of course they aren't. *That something's difficult must be another reason to do it.* Maybe I've already made my decision. Do you know why they say I'm a dangerous pick? Why some people say I won't even go in the top ten? It's not because of the knees or the ankles or my back. It's because they can see the lack of passion for the game. They can see my hesitation. And it doesn't bother me, really. I've heard it all my life, all of the comparisons to Kwame Brown and Olowokandi. The only thing that bothers me is deep down I think they're right—and they're *still* counting on me to make them boatloads of money. You can't teach size, but you can't teach ambition either. I put in the hours when I was a kid 'cause I didn't have anything else. But these past few years have been different . . ."

"But you were player of the year . . ."

"So were Adam Morrison and JJ Redick. Not that they didn't try, but if I'm not willing to work hard enough to stay in the conversation? Well, it's a waste of my time and their energy."

"And a whole lot of money . . ."

"Fuck the money, Slim! This is about my life. Talent can disappear—the only way to be great is to work at it. So if basketball's the easy choice versus the right one? Well shit. What if I get lazy? What if after a few years of making money I become a depressed jackass who dreams about what he could have become? If it isn't what inspires me to get up every morning, or if it just becomes the reason I take sleeping pills each night? I don't want to live for my vacation days. And that's what scares me, that's where I feel the dread: basketball's the easy choice, but is it the right one?"

"Well, like you said, you've already made the decision. We're driving to the NBA. But as a thought experiment, what would happen if you quit? You'd be the laughing stock of the entire sports world. They're going to call you out. They'll say you're a disgrace to children's dreams, that you're spitting in the face of all those players who couldn't make it, that you're a coward for abandoning basketball to make Philly cheesesteaks. Can you imagine being ridiculed and pestered and criticized for years? The laughing stock of the sports nation. You want to be the target again? You saw how I was treated when I came back from Iraq. Even sacrificing your life for your country doesn't exempt you from that shit . . ."

"Since when have I made decisions based on what other people will think? I'd be a coward if I were afraid of being called a coward. Of course I'll get ridiculed. But why will it be hard? I don't watch the news and I don't go to malls and I don't read *People Magazine* and I don't keep up with the NBA. I feel most alive around you and when I'm in the kitchen. That's the truth, and I don't want to leave it. Who cares about all the noise outside? And in a couple of months when it's all died down—'cause, let's be honest, who really gives a shit about college athletes?—they'll make a documentary about how it all went wrong except that it won't work 'cause I won't be sad or depressed. They'll realize their dream wasn't mine. They'll be upset that I didn't fulfill *their dream*, that I didn't inspire a heartfelt documentary. And then they'll forget me like they've forgotten you. I can't control what others think, I can only be responsible for my own opinion of myself. And isn't that part of what it means to be an adult? To be true to yourself? To make that decision? To have conviction in what you believe in? Jordan retired twice *despite* all the ridicule. And now he's considered the greatest 'cause he was honest with himself despite all the bullshit."

"We're talking about MJ now? 'Cause if you're talking about quitting basketball, he isn't exactly the best example . . ."

The Beast shook his head. "But that's where you're wrong, Slim. This is exactly about him. Sports heroes always transcend the game. Do you know what happened in Jordan's second year?"

"Let me guess . . . won everything there was to win. Dropped sixty in a game—"

"He broke his foot. Missed sixty-four games. Jerry Reinsdorf, the Bull's owner, told him not to risk coming back too early. Had his whole career in front of him, he said. Get healthy before next season. And when Jordan still insisted, Reinsdorf asked him a question: You've got a piercing headache, you can't even see straight. And in front of you are ten painkillers, one of which is coated in cyanide. Do you take the risk?"

"What'd Jordan do, get up and leave?"

"He said it depends on how bad of a headache. And a couple weeks later he set a playoff scoring record that still stands to this day. Sixty-three points against Larry Bird in Boston Garden. Not to mention McHale and Parish and Johnson. Passion overrides everything. That's what I'm saying. And that's just one story. You've heard about 'The Flu Game'?"

"Alright, well, I get it. A fucking phenom. LeBron isn't any different—"

"Have some respect, Slim. LeBron and Jordan belong in separate conversations."

"Okay, whatever. But this doesn't explain why you wouldn't go to the NBA. If you want my opinion, it's only reinforcing my argument: I'm not calling you out, Hugh, but you can't afford to leave the game."

The Beast shook his head. "You're not listening. Look." The Beast grabbed a napkin and hunched over the kitchen island. "Can I have a pen, Lockart? Here. In Jordan's first *nine years*—eight, really, because he missed most of his second year—here's what he did. Also, Lockart, would you mind grabbing me another beer?"

The burgers began to sizzle. The Beast was determined as he wrote, like a curious student in the classroom.

THE FIRST NINE YEARS

Rookie of the Year

2 Olympic golds

2 slam dunk championships

'88 DPOY

All-defensive 1st Team '88–'93

All-star '85–'93 (never <u>wasn't</u> an All-Star)

Scoring Champ '87–'93

3 MVPs ('88, '91, '92)

3 Championships

3 Finals MVPs

"The first nine years. And he did all of this, *all of it*, before he was thirty," The Beast said. "Now you can look at this and think yeah-okay-he-was-a-great-player-maybe-the-greatest-of-all-time-big-deal-okay. Chamberlain was also legendary. So was Bill Russell. And Magic and Kobe and LeBron. But this is why Jordan beats them all. It's not because of this napkin or all the other napkins I'd need to write his heroics down. Because heroics can't be quantified—legends can't be reduced to a piece of paper. Even though he is the GOAT (That means the Greatest of All Time, Lockart), the reason Jordan is a hero has almost nothing to do with basketball. In 1993—"

"You mean, after the first three-peat?" Slim cut in. "Man, that definitely was legendary. He had to go through Thomas and Dumars and Wilkins and Bird and Magic and Price and Daugherty and Drexler and Ewing and Starks and Jordan Rules and Chuck Daly and Pat Riley.

Fuck. Not to mention facing off against Barkley. He was a giant killer, I get it. Okay. Point taken. But you're saying there's something else . . ."

"You're still talking about the game of basketball, Slim. Listen: Jordan's dad was the most important person in his life. He wasn't just his father, but his mentor, his best friend. For every championship he was there with the champagne. And in the summer of '93, after the third championship, Jordan's dad, James, was murdered on the highway in his brand new car. Robbed and shot in the Lexus Michael had bought him as a championship present. Two months later, Jordan retired from the game. And that was just the catalyst. It would've happened anyway. He was forced to question his passion for the game. And, of course, conspiracy theories started about how James was assassinated, about MJ's supposed gambling problem, about his ties to the mafia—anything for a story. And when the media tried to profit, how do you think the most famous person in the world responded? He questioned. And for that, he had to step away from basketball. See, his dad always told him he could do anything he set his mind to, and the bottom line was Jordan needed a change. A chapter had ended, albeit in a horrific way; but it was time to move on to something else, and Jordan had an idea. His father had always thought Michael should try professional baseball—not 'cause he'd be great but 'cause it'd be a challenge. *That something's difficult must be another reason to do it.* He'd played baseball in high school but abandoned it for basketball. And so when his dad died, Michael decided to take a chance. He wanted to remember what it was to play for the love of the game."

"You're saying he didn't enjoy it any more?" I asked.

"I'm saying it was no longer a challenge. Someone once said he wasn't addicted to gambling, he was addicting to competing. Even before his dad died, Jordan had been struggling to find that passion. In '93 he couldn't imagine what was next. When it came to basketball, there was nothing else. And so in Phil Jackson's office, Jordan broke down in tears trying to come up with an answer. He'd won championships and MVPs and defensive awards and gold medals. He couldn't think of a worthy challenge to keep playing the game. And neither could Phil, the greatest coach of all time. He also knew that Jordan had already proven he was the greatest. So where do you go from there? Where do you go when you're empty?"

"Moral of the story—don't succeed," Slim said wittily.

"No, success isn't linear, Slim. He'd lost his passion for the game. But the hero started to emerge because he had the courage to step away. Not because it was a wise choice professionally, but because it was a wise choice existentially. And he went and tried baseball—one of the hardest sports in the world to play well—a sport he hadn't played since high school, and he failed miserably. *Jordan Rides the Bus.* Amazing documentary. He struck out, he dropped balls, he was the laughing stock of the entire sports world. They said he was a joke, a fraud, an over-hyped athlete seeking attention, saying he'd quit 'cause of gambling problems, that he was using his celebrity to undermine the game. They said it was a marketing ploy for an egomaniac, a selfish businessman hogging the spotlight . . . but instead of listening to all the noise, Jordan kept playing. Day in and day out he practiced. Scouts say he was the most driven player on the team. And soon he began to show signs of not only holding his own but *succeeding.* After months of errors and strikeouts and criticism, the same journalists that had ridiculed him were now starting to watch in awe, writing columns about his success. But Jordan didn't care. He wasn't there to prove them wrong. He was there to prove something to himself. In that year he faced more criticism than an entire family faces in a century, but he kept his head held high 'cause he found what he was looking for. He didn't want to be the best, he wanted to be passionate. Before he ever became a star, before he was rejected from the JV team, he'd played sports because he loved them, plain and simple. Out there in the backyard, that's where he found love; and by refusing to become a washed-up player who slowly watched his passion fade away, Jordan retired in '93 'cause he knew a life without passion isn't a life worth living. And then you know the rest . . . he came back full of love. A year and a half later he joined the Bulls in the playoffs and came back in incredible form. Fifty-five points in Madison Square Garden. But it wasn't immediate: against Orlando he committed two critical turnovers that cost the Bulls the series. And just a side note: everyone was shocked that Jordan *didn't win* that year. Do you know how ridiculous that is? That they expected him to just come back and win immediately? Well, he didn't take long. But what do you think they said at first? Everyone attacked him, said it wasn't meant to be. Maybe number 45 could never match number 23. And sure, he was pissed and disappointed, but he'd also found what he was looking for. It's not about talent, it's about the motivation. And the following season he became a part of the greatest team in sports history. Seventy-two wins in eighty-two games. That's unheard of. That's just stupid. Not to mention winning three more championships and countless other accolades. Now tell me, Slim, if you can see—"

"Well, I can't argue with that. And yeah, Jordan was and is The Man. But—"

"Hold on, there's something else. Have another beer. So Jordan retired a second time. The shot over Russell? Everyone said *that was the image*, The Last Shot, a final image of brilliance. But we all made the mistake of thinking he was done; we all made the mistake of wanting the dream to end as we saw fit. But Jordan isn't a myth and he doesn't give a shit about what we think. So he came back. Again. This time in a Wizards' uniform. What the hell is he doing, we said.

Who the hell are the Wizards? And although we were excited, most of us were kind of sad because it wasn't a fairy-tale ending. But he wasn't there to read us bedtime stories. Once again, he was there to prove something to himself, not us. And so even if he'd failed and sat on the bench, it still would've been heroic for him to return to the game. But this is Michael Jordan. He's the only forty-year-old player in history to score forty-plus points in a game. He's also the oldest player in history to score fifty points in a game. And he was *the only player* in 2002 to play all eighty-two games . . . a forty-year old man outplaying teenagers for an entire season! And here's the icing on the cake. In the end, he disappointed us. Did you see his Hall of Fame speech? Michael Jordan isn't a myth. He is flawed, like everyone. He wants to win with the Bobcats and is failing miserably. And that's what it takes if you want to pursue passion. It means sacrificing everything, including your own ego, in pursuit of the capital-T Truth about the game."

"And what's that?" I asked.

"If you listen closely," The Beast was brimming, "to the video in '98, Game Six, Jordan hugs Phil and says, 'I had faith, I had faith.' And that's what matters. That's why I question my love for the game. Jordan believed in spite of it all. He sacrificed everything. It's like I said: sports heroes always transcend the game."

We would've liked to digest what felt like The Beast's speech, but the burgers were starting to burn. "The olive oil!" Slim yelped. "It's popping all over the place." The pan sizzled as Slim cracked two eggs and stood back. They expanded towards each other; Slim kept the spatula between them. Meanwhile, I took the burgers off the stove and The Beast, using a folded cooking towel, pulled the pan of potatoes from the oven, tilting it ever so slightly above the plates to slide the ingredients off. After serving all the potatoes 'cause he knew we'd want seconds, he left a collection of onions amid the caramel juices as he went over to the kitchen sink. He ripped a paper towel off the dispenser and returned to wipe each plate.

"The beauty's in the details," The Beast said. He double-checked that each plate was clean before pouring the rest of the baking pan's caramel sauce atop the potatoes.

"Speaking of sports heroes, Hugh, did you see the Bo Jackson *30 for 30*? That man's a goddamn legend . . . a modern-day Zeus," Slim said.

"A man's man, for sure," The Beast replied as he wiped the plates again. "Actually, yeah, I've wanted to ask you that for a while: what do you think it means to be a man, really? And I'm not talking about some bullshit notion of biceps, cigars, and whiskey."

"Being a man is what we're doing: cooking and philosophizing and drinking whiskey." Slim cracked the third egg into the now sizzling frying pan. He was careful not to break the yolk, pouring the eggs in slowly in a small puddle next to the others so they'd cook individually.

"No I mean more like an adjective. Not one . . . let's say three."

"An adjective?" Slim said. "That's easy. Respect. Self-respect."

"You're going to need to elaborate . . ."

The Beast placed a toasted burger bun on each plate. Slim kept an eye on the eggs as they began to bubble and brown at the corners. "I mean *self-respect*, plain and simple," Slim continued. "'Cause how do you expect to respect someone—or be respected by anyone, for that matter—if you aren't able to respect yourself? A world without respect? That's not a world I want to live in."

"Fair enough. I wouldn't put that first though," The Beast said. "Self-respect can turn into arrogance. You respect yourself too much and you start looking down on other people. Then it turns into the opposite of what you're talking about, right?"

The Beast placed a piece of lettuce on each bun and asked me to pass him the coleslaw. He packed it down on top of the lettuce with the rounded edge of a spoon.

"Well, you just gotta be mature about it," Slim said. "I didn't know these adjectives were ranked. I have to say which one I'm putting first, now? I thought you wanted my opinion."

"Well no, you're right, they don't have to be ranked. But my first choice is honesty. And I'm not just talking about honesty and having good morals and what not . . . I mean, sure, you've got morality as part of it too, but it also means being honest with yourself."

"But now you're talking about conviction."

"No, that's more about feeling convinced. Take integrity, which also means honesty. In Latin, what is it? The *quality of being whole*—comes from *integer*, entire."

"Here we go, Lockart!" Slim laughed. "Hugh's always trying to impress me with his Latin roots and shit. You think the origin matters? I don't give a flying fuck where in the hell the word came from as long as I understand it—"

"You know as well as I do that's just wrong," The Beast replied. "Origins are everything."

"Well, not in the present! I don't need a Latin lesson to understand what you're talking about."

"What about the second adjective then?"

"That's easy. Toughness." Slim used the spatula to carefully flip each egg. "A man who isn't tough? Life will break you. Better men than you and me have seen some heavy shit. You ever read that DFW article about John McCain? I mean, how it really happened? Maybe the toughest dude there is—"

"Yeah, but that's a perfect example because you didn't vote for him. Toughness can't be the only quality . . . you've gotta be able to see the bigger picture. I mean, there are plenty of people who endured pain 'cause they were tough, but it doesn't mean they were good people. I'd go with determination, being able to stick to a task, believing in yourself. But once again, check out the root. Give me shit, I don't care. It's Latin for limiting something, fixing something, setting boundaries. You have to know your limits. Determine your boundaries. You're the judge. Have to be able to make decisions and stick to them."

Slim flipped an egg on its yolk. "Fucking Latin . . . what did you take, three semesters? Prefixes and suffixes . . . no need to get all fancy. I understand what it means: determination. And it's a good one, too. But I'd still take toughness. You can be determined as shit, but if you aren't tough? Good luck when the bullets start flying." He turned the stove off and moved the frying pan off the burner. "You know where I'd be without toughness, Hugh? I'd be in an Iraqi sewer. Or maybe hung up and tortured like one of them Blackwater idiots. Or, but wait, they changed the name, didn't they?"

"Xe."

"Zee?"

"Xe."

"See?"

"X-e. Xe."

"Well, whatever, they're idiots. Erik Prince is a piece of shit," Slim said. "That man deserves to be bitch-slapped and locked up. But no, Hugh, you've gotta be tough if you want to be a man. There's no way around it."

"Agree to disagree." The Beast laid two tomato slices on each of our mounting burgers. "So I've got honesty and determination. And you've got self-respect and toughness. What about the third one?"

I placed a square of American cheese atop the burgers and slid the pan with the buns into the oven.

"Well," Slim said. "I should've put this up at the top: loyalty. That's everything. More important than being tough, better than honesty. It's number one. Without loyalty I'd be nowhere, 'cause loyalty also means to yourself. My father—whoever the fuck he is or was—wasn't loyal for shit. He pussed out and left me alone to be raised by Wilhelmina. But you know why I stuck around? Why I stuck it out with the moms and then Stoke Ridge? Why I stayed in that shitty trailer instead of peacing out and becoming some kind of drug king-pin? And don't pretend like I couldn't have done it either! It's not like I liked it down at Stoke Ridge. See, I thought Dykes was loyal to me, but he was just loyal to the idea. Real loyalty means you stick with it. You can call it determination . . . you can give me the Latin root if you really feel like it, but I'm talking bout being loyal to something bigger than yourself. Loyalty to the idea that you or I can make it."

Slim took the frying pan off the stove and walked the eggs over to the burgers. "Now put the burger on first. Just nice like that. And Hugh, you got the avocados? Ohhhh baby. I'm about to be loyal to this burger! Better believe it! We're almost done now that we've got the eggs on top. They'll be in the oven just a hot minute."

The fried eggs fit like puzzle pieces on top of the second burger patty. "All that's left is the condiments. But we'll do that at the bar. Lockart? Can you bring the other half of the bun?" Slim asked. "The cheese will melt a bit more with the egg, you can take those out of the oven now."

"Here, for the integrity," The Beast pierced each burger with a steak knife, down the center.

"Loyalty's good," The Beast said as we carried our plates from the kitchen to the bar. "But I'm thinking humility. And just 'cause I know you love it, Slim, I'll tell you about the root. *Humus*, the idea of earthbound. Literally, low to the ground, *down to earth*. If you want to be a man, you better be humble. So I've got honesty, determination, and humility, and you've got respect, toughness, and loyalty. I like it. Not bad. What about you, Lockart?"

We were sitting at the bar. I was to the side of Slim and The Beast. Slim, on my far side, opened his burger and placed the knife next to his plate. He splashed on Texas Pete.

"I don't abide by hot sauce," I said.

"No, I mean, to be a man . . ." The Beast clarified.

"You know Jane has this saying, she calls it the three Ps: patience, passion, and how to be present."

I lifted the burger off the plate and took my first bite. For a while, despite the hurricane, only the sound of chewing filled the bar.

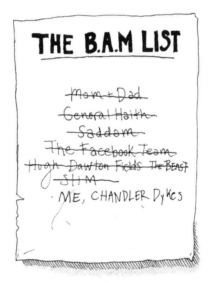

17

I don't remember which song was playing, only Slim's Famous Burger and the quiet. Despite the alcohol and the weed, we took small bites. Slim and The Beast didn't speak. We rarely looked up from our plates, occasionally resurfacing for a sip of beer or water.

"One of the best Boys' Nights yet!" Slim exclaimed. The Beast smiled. And then out of the churning skies high above a thunderous *BOOM* struck the bar.

The serenity disappeared along with the lights. Slim shoved The Beast and I to the ground as if he were back in Iraq. He told us to cover our heads, instinctively crawling on his forearms. The bar quaked and the lights flickered. A seam in the sky ripped in two, pouring white light all around. Sheets of rain floated across the parking lot. The floodwaters eddied on the churning ground, reflecting Beverly's gyrations high above. The pine trees contorted and buckled and twisted; the bushes tried to keep their heads above water, their windswept leaves revealing skeletal cores.

"Holy shit," The Beast said after moving to the front door. "Look at my jeep." The tires were sinking or the water was rising—either way, a sizable tree branch was weighing the Jeep down. It stuck out of the passenger window, dark and grotesque. Other debris slammed into the car and fell by the wayside like wreckage.

"Goddammit!" The Beast cursed. "The windows are still open! I gotta get my bag out of there before it's too late."

"Are you serious, Hugh? Who gives a shit about the bag? Look outside!" Slim screamed. "Those are gale-force winds . . . you're not about to risk your life!"

The wind dislodged the Jeep's wheels from the muddied ground. It began to slide ever so slightly across the flooded parking lot. "I've gotta get it, Slim. You don't understand. I'll close the windows, that's it—"

"Brother, wait it out. The eye's going to come soon enough. Look at the clouds, Hugh. Just wait a second."

We could no longer reflect. The white noise of the rain was like a cocoon. Beverly consumed everything in her path. A rogue mailbox flew into the scene and smashed one of the Jeep's side-mirrors. The Beast took a step forward.

"Hugh, don't go out just yet." I held him back. "You're going to get yourself killed." He ignored my advice.

"God dammit Hugh . . . don't be a fucking idiot!" Slim yelled.

Another tree branch penetrated the Jeep's rear cabin. "I'm going Slim. Come with me. It'll just take a second."

Beer awaited inside the bar. Our burgers remained half-eaten. But in an instant Slim and The Beast were laboring in the gale, crouching like war photographers, sticking their arms out for balance. They grabbed onto each other's hands as they turned their backs to the wind. Walking sideways, they battled the hurricane's fury. Their broad shoulders deflected leaves, small trees and branches. As they made their way across the brown, swamped ground, rain swirled around them like sand in the desert. Although the Jeep wasn't more than one hundred feet away, it took them a few minutes to reach it. The Beast fumbled with his keys and finally jumped into the driver's seat. I could barely make out Slim's silhouette within the torrential rain, but he was on the other side now, struggling with a tree branch. When the taillights shone orange, Slim heaved the trees' remnants into the howling air. Slim opened the door behind The Beast and for a moment they just sat. Once the backseat windows were rolled up, Slim and The Beast emerged and headed back towards the bar. Slim crouched low to the ground. The Beast clutched his bag to his chest. And then, all of a sudden, a patch of blue sky seeped out. Light emerged behind the tree line. Just like that the howling stopped. They were caught in the perfect still, dumbfounded, squinting into the eye of the storm. The Beast put his arm around Slim and began plodding back to the bar, sloshing in puddles of mud like a rubber-booted kid. By the time they reached the front door it seemed Beverly had disappeared: no more thunder or lightning, only a gentle breeze. Slim and The Beast laughed. Branches settled into the mud. The pines stood up, shaking off the rain, stretching their branches. The worst was still to come, and yet everything was calm. All three of us were like boys who'd just witnessed a magic trick. I stepped outside to join them and marvel at the scene: despite the calm, the churning wall of the eye still loomed in the distance. "Not over yet, boys. We've got some burgers and beer waiting!" The Beast kept his arm around Slim's shoulder as they headed back inside.

Just before returning, with burgers on our mind, we saw a shadowy figure emerge in the distance. A man began sprinting towards us with alarming speed. He came from the forest's edge armed with a shotgun.

The yellow-toothed smile said it all. "It's time for dinner, Slim. What are we having?"

"Take it easy, man," The Beast didn't know who it was.

Slim stepped forward. "Get back, Hugh, it's Dykes."

"So you've told him about me!" Dykes said. "Well isn't that nice. Maybe we could all be friends! That is, if you have room for me, faggots."

Dykes lead us inside with the barrel of the shotgun. We could take him, I felt Slim thinking. I whispered, "Don't do anything rash."

Back in the bar Dykes poked at The Beast's chest with his gun. "Sit down, on the stool. I've been waiting for you, Hugh. Or should I call you Beast? That's what you are."

"What the fuck are you doing, Dykes?" Slim regained his composure.

"Now now, be patient, Slim. All in good time."

"Chandler, please. You've—"

"Shut up, Lockart. I'm tired of hearing your shit. Sit there, yeah, next to him. You too, Slim. And take off your shirt while you're at it."

Slim laughed. "You've got to be kidding me, Dykes! You're still a fucking freak. You'll have to shoot me first. Go ahead. You don't have the balls . . ."

"YOU WILL DO AS YOU'RE TOLD, SON! TAKE IT OFF! NOW!"

"Slim," The Beast spoke softly. "Just do it. It's not worth getting shot at."

"What's that, Beast? What are you saying to your friend? Why don't you take your shirt off, too. Yeah, just like that. Maybe get on your knees, too."

Slim and The Beast reluctantly removed their T-shirts. All of their muscles were contracted. The Beast got on his knees in front of the bar.

"Oooh, look at you," Dykes said as he poked at Slim's pecks with the gun. "You've been keeping up with the regimen, haven't you? You used to be such a good cadet . . ."

"What the fuck is this, Dykes?" Slim swiped at the gun. Dykes recoiled. "This is between us, not them," Slim pleaded.

"WHAT is between us, Slim? WHAT, exactly? Don't you mean this is between *him*?" Dykes pointed at The Beast. "Now you're thinking. You fucking faggot."

Dykes was as drunk as I'd ever seen him, but there was a fury in his eyes that none of us could understand. He ripped a piece of paper out of his pocket and waved it in front of The Beast's face.

"Your friend here has been lying to you, Slim. Don't you want to know what happened? Don't you want to ask him about Coach Brees? Why he was sent to The Skillet? How almost killing a man went unpunished? Why you're driving a piece of shit Jeep instead of flying to Milwaukee? ASK HIM!"

"What the fuck are you talking about, Dykes? You're insane. I'm not asking him shit. Hugh, don't answer him."

"Beast? Why don't you tell him? I know your secret. You're a coward and a deserter *and* a faggot. GET UP."

"Hugh, don't answer him. Don't give him the satisfaction."

Dykes shrieked and shoved the gun into The Beast's face. "FINE! I'LL DO IT MYSELF, LIKE ALWAYS. Get on your knees, Beast! Get back down! Or no, why don't you do the honors, Mr. Barman?"

Dykes slammed the paper on the bar and placed the barrel on my chest. Our plates were still steaming. "READ IT!" Dykes bellowed.

I unfolded the piece of paper but refused to answer to the sergeant. "I have no business with this. You'll have to read it yourself, Chandler."

Just a hint of fear flashed across his face. Even when he had a shotgun, none of us would answer to him. "I'll do it myself. You're right, it's better like that. You know I had a nice little chat with Coach Brees the other day, Beast. He was mighty interested in that interview you gave . . . seemed to be able to read between the lines.

Don't want to go to the NBA, do you? Trying to get out of it? I did a bit of detective work myself, wondering why you were driving up to the draft."

The Beast remained calm, but something flickered in his eyes.

"What the hell are you talking about?" Slim asked.

"Slim, it's fine," The Beast responded.

"You're damn right it's fine!" Dykes yelled. "Well maybe not for you. Coach Brees's lawyer is good, you know. Very good indeed. He has all the answers. I just had to figure out how to talk to him. What's in the bag, Beast? Why don't you ask him, Slim? He's trying to run away. He's a coward, that's all."

The Beast remained silent.

"What the hell are you talking about, Dykes?" Slim asked.

"Don't ask me. Ask him. He bought two tickets. He's a faggot. The private detective said you tried to buy two tickets out of the country with cash. But you can't do that, can you, Beast? These are different times. Still have mommy and daddy's credit card though. Do you miss them? How sad. All that education and you forgot they can track the credit card . . ."

"Hugh?" Slim asked. "What is he talking about?"

"There you go," Dykes said. "You should've asked him all along."

The Beast had nothing to say.

"Seems your friend here is afraid to talk," Dykes sniggered. "I guess I'll speak for him. Just like always. You weren't going to take I-40 through Greensboro, were you, Beast? You were planning to flee to Atlanta. An international flight."

Slim furrowed his brow skeptically. The Beast was visibly tense.

"Don't want to tell him, do you, Beast?" Dykes prodded. "What are you, embarrassed? I'll tell him by myself then. Beast here signed a contract. Back when he punched Coach Brees he was facing jail time.

He didn't tell you that? Did you really believe he could get away with community service? He's a liar. He cut a deal with the judge—twelve percent of earnings on a future NBA contract. That way Brees could get paid for the damages. It's expensive to almost die. Not to mention psychological problems. Brees has been keeping an eye on him, hired a private investigator. But I've been following you too, Slim. What a coincidence! What are the odds? Your friend here isn't allowed to leave North Carolina—also part of the contract. Not until after the draft at least. He wasn't invited to Milwaukee. He has to stay inside the state until draft day, when he signs with a team. And then Coach Brees can reap twelve percent of the profits! But you don't want to sign, do you Beast? What are you, scared? You're nothing without your nickname. You're nothing more than a stupid ballplayer, that's all. What, did you think that Brees would forget about it? That you could get out of paying him? All that education, and for what? Why did you sign it then? Too scared to face criminal charges? The only reason he's with you, Slim, is 'cause he's using you to get out of town. Do you know what will happen if they catch him? You'll be tried as an accomplice. Twelve percent of an NBA contract—this is America we're talking about. They'll be looking for you for years. And you thought I was the problem! The big powerful Beast, signing away his name instead of being a man and facing jail time. And now you're trying to get out of it! That's where you're wrong. Your friend here, Slim, he chose to sign the dotted line. A slave to the system. Part of the problem. What does that make you then, Beast? What do we call a man who signs his freedom away? And now you're fleeing? Now you're reneging? That sounds like cowardice to me, doesn't it? And what about you, Slim? What does that make you? Some kind of hostage? He used you Slim . . . he lied to you from the beginning. And you thought he was honest! Why do you think he made you his 'agent'—I bet you never signed any documents. He was going to abandon you, Slim, just like Coach Brees, just like your father . . ."

For a moment it seemed as if Slim's anger was shifting to his friend.

"Slim," The Beast explained. "I wasn't trying to use you, I promise. I got our tickets out of the car . . ."

Dykes smiled.

"No, Hugh." Slim took a deep breath. "It doesn't matter. I forgive you. Don't give this coward the satisfaction. Right now, we need to deal with this piece of shit. Later we can talk about it."

Slim stepped between his best friend and Sgt. Dykes. Slim told The Beast to stand up. "Your plan didn't work, Dykes. You fucking jackass. What did you think? That I was going to come back to you? That I was going to make Hugh the problem? You still don't get it, do you? You never got it. It doesn't matter. You're a pathetic piece of shit. Either shoot me or get the fuck out!"

And with that, Slim grabbed the shotgun barrel and held it tight to his own chest. "You're going to shoot me? Is that how this goes down? I don't think you'll do it. *You're* the goddamn coward. You think you can come in here with a piece of paper and take away all that's happened? Go on then, pull the trigger. I'm not going to stop you."

Dykes's eyes flickered as if someone inside had lit a match. In the next instant he pumped the shotgun and pulled the trigger. The gun went *click*. But no bullets came out. Just a hollow, defeated silence. Slim laughed as he yanked the shotgun from Dykes's grasp. He threw it across the room. "We're going to need some rope, Lockart."

Slim took one swing and knocked Dykes to the ground. "Can't even load a shotgun correctly." Slim turned around.

Dykes stood up. The Beast held his friend back. Clutching his bleeding face, the sergeant blinked stupidly at the three of us. He pressed his hands to his eyes and touched the back of his bloodied head. He looked at his palm and wiped it on his khakis, which turned a brownish red. He raised his hands like a boxer and looked around wildly for a weapon. He settled on a steak knife beside the burgers.

"Don't you fucking touch my burger!" Slim picked up a barstool and cocked it behind his head.

But The Beast remained in front of Slim, preventing him from attacking. Dykes began to advance slowly. He fumbled to keep his balance and clutched the side of the bar, taking hold of one of the plates on the countertop, crashing it to the ground. "You can't protect him, Hugh Dawton-Fields. Just like your parents."

The Beast's eyes widened. "What did you say to me?"

"I said you can't protect him. Just like your parents in that fire."

Dykes pointed at The Beast with the serrated knife. "Stop hiding behind your boyfriend, Slim. For old times sake get down on the ground. DROP AND GIVE ME TWENTY! Come around where daddy can see you. I should've fucked you when I had the chance, you fucking faggot."

Slim dropped the bar stool and charged. Neither The Beast nor I could hold him back. All three fell to the ground. In a matter of seconds the scuffle was over. Dykes was unconscious on the blood-stained floor, gushing profusely from the head. Slim stood up and brushed himself off. He gave one last kick to Dykes's body. "Hugh, we got him."

But The Beast was clutching his torso, writhing on the floor.

"Hugh?" Slim dropped to his knees. "Hugh, what the fuck happened!"

"Slim." The Beast looked down at the steak knife lodged deep in his chest. He tried to sit up but couldn't manage. Slim placed one hand under his friend's head.

"Don't look at it, brother, you're fine."

The Beast coughed up blood. "Slim? What happened?" He tried to prop himself up on his elbows but fell back down again. "Slim, listen to me. I want—"

"No, Hugh, don't talk like—"

"SLIM. *Please listen.* I was going to tell you. I promise I was. I just wanted to get out of North Carolina first, to leave UNC and all the rest of it. I bought a ticket for you, too. It was time to move on . . ."

"Don't talk, Hugh, you're fine. Lockart's calling an ambulance."

"I was planning to tell you, Slim. I'm sorry. I didn't mean to—"

The Beast's eyes widened. He coughed up blood. "Slim? What's happening?"

There were tears coming down Slim's face. "You're fine, brother. Don't worry." He caressed his friend's forehead. "You're fine, Hugh, it's nothing. You just stay right there. Are you with me? The ambulance is coming. We're going to be all right, I promise. Just keep breathing. Just like that. LOCKART! WHERE'S THE AMBULANCE!" He wiped his eyes. "That's it, brother. We're gonna be fine. Just keep pressing. Just like that. We're gonna be fine, brother."

No ambulance was coming. Beverly had started up again. The Beast began to breathe heavily, watching the sunlight disappear from the bar. "It's like those snow globes when you're a kid," he said. Dust particles danced and glowed in the bar. Slim looked at me with pleading eyes, but he knew there'd be no siren. "You just stay right there, Hugh. You're fine. You're fine Hugh. Don't worry."

The Beast was serene. "This is it, isn't it?"

"No, brother, stop talking. You're going to be fine, just deep breaths."

"Slim," The Beast whispered. "Just listen."

For a moment only silence. Nothing but a calm breeze. Then the rain patter on the roof. Soon the thunder and lightning began. The Beast whispered as he pulled his best friend close to his face. "It's okay Slim. Just listen."

The eye of the storm passed onwards, making way for the screaming wind. The Beast exhaled and closed his eyes. For a moment, Slim remained draped over his friend. Seconds later, he'd gone into the breach.

EPILOGUE

They put The Beast in a body bag and Sgt. Dykes in a straitjacket. When they searched Chandler's cabin they found a rabid opossum that was quickly put down. They put the B.A.M. LIST in a plastic bag and labeled it EVIDENCE. Only one name at the bottom wasn't crossed off:

THE B.A.M. LIST
~~MOM + DAD~~
~~GENERAL HAITH~~
~~SADDAM~~
~~THE FACEBOOK TEAM~~
~~HUGH DAWTON-FIELDS, THE BEAST~~
~~SLIM~~
ME, CHANDLER DYKES

Hugh Dawton-Fields was cremated in the Chapel Hill morgue. His jersey now hangs up in UNC's rafters. An award-winning sports documentary entitled *The Beast* tells quite the tragic story of an NBA-career that could've been. Sports fans throughout the nation were shocked by the tragedy, but only those who come to Lockart's know what really happened. Those who make the pilgrimage to try Slim's Famous Burger always ask about the man behind it all.

"He's out there somewhere," I respond. But after telling Slim's story, I ask *them* the question. Your guess is as good as mine, I say, 'cause the plain and simple truth is no one has seen or heard from him since. Some of the media likes to pretend he had something to do with the killing; others say he went to England to get his Ph.D. Some say he's in California selling drugs and drinking whiskey, while some think Sgt. Dykes hired a former cadet to fulfill the B.A.M. LIST. And then some people say he traveled abroad with a free airline ticket, or that he committed suicide 'cause there was no Slim without The Beast. Whatever the case, he left in Hugh's Jeep. Everything else is just opinion. But there's a whole lot more to a man than his upbringing, or even his history, and certainly more to his story than a bartender can surmise. So I tell those who come in, usually over a glass of whiskey: wherever he is, whoever he wanted to be, well, I can only speak of Slim and The Beast. But it's strange, I tell them. As I watched Hugh Dawton-Fields lying in a pool of his own blood, all I could think of was that half-eaten burger. Lettuce, coleslaw, sliced tomatoes, a burger patty, American cheese, avocados, a second patty, a fried egg, ketchup and hot sauce, Texas Pete to be precise.

There's only one burger on the menu—home fries and glazed onions come on the side. In the daytime, cooking with Jane, Lockart's Bar becomes Lockart's Restaurant. We all want to feel part of something real, something sacred, something profound. Like Slim once told me, we all want to feel part of a tribe. In the past but not forgotten. Eternal, somehow. So when simple routines go to plan and everything else goes to waste, we can finally breathe. And when we feel at ease, on those nights we let our guard down, when to love a man is to be a man and not the other way around, well, I don't want to live in Slim and The Beast's past, but I want their past to live in me.

H.A.M. LIST
(THE HEROES ACCORDING TO ME LIST)

Slim and The Beast *was made possible in part by the following heroes who backed the book on Inkshares.com. Thank you.*

Aaron Lopez-Barrantes
Alexander C Miles
Andrea L. Blickman
Ann F. Gordon
Anthony L. Clay
Ari D. Gross
Barbara D. McManus
Chris Garafola
Damien McKeon
Dan Fitz
David Deaton
David H. Eil
Deborah Gross
Elaine Sciolino
Ellen Hemphill
Erin McGee
Frances Fitz Gaines
Gabriella Zavatti
Gillian M. Dolce
Ian Jagel
Jaybird O'Berski

Jean Paul Guizol
Johannes Theron
Johnathan L Boursiquot
Joshua Mangiagli
Kathleen Schenley
Kathryn G. Hemphill
Kathy & Brad Morgan
L. Richardson Preyer III
Laura Frankstone
Lex Organ
Lucile Taillade
M.J. Holding
Marc Rubin
Marilyn Jacobs Preyer
Mary Kathryn Hemphill
Matthew Rubin
Maurice W. Boswell
Michael D. Hanas
Monika Margaret Raithel
Monique Bamford
Niamh Quinn

Nicholas Fraser
Nor Hall & Roger Hale
Pam Freedman
Parker Jacobs Preyer
Peggy Bouveret
Paul D. Spence
Rafael Lopez Barrantes
Raphaelle Costes
Roger L. Hale
Ronald Strom
Seth Nichols
Shirley Drechsel
Siddharth Rao
Stephen Snyder
Steve Hemphill
Steven J. Levine
Todd Hemphill
Victor Saez Lopez-Barrantes
Wesley Spence
Zachary Press
Zachary Strom